She had to leave the man she loved

Catherine anxiously watched the rider approach—a tall straight figure on a pale horse, his head held proudly. Don Jaime was returning home.

Quickly Catherine drew back into the shadows, pained at the thought of leaving Soria...of leaving Jaime. She brushed against the floss-silk tree as she suddenly moved toward him, a scatter of pale pink blossoms falling at her feet.

Jaime dismounted, then stood looking intently down at her. For one blinding moment she thought he was about to kiss her. She could almost feel the touch of his lips on hers....But instead he put his hands gently on her shoulders, turning her to face the light.

"When my employees are dishonest," he said unexpectedly, "they destroy themselves—and me."

JEAN S. MacLEOD
is also the author of these
Harlequin Romances

Meeting in Madrid

by

JEAN S. MacLEOD

Harlequin Books

TORONTO • LONDON • LOS ANGELES • AMSTERDAM
SYDNEY • HAMBURG • PARIS • STOCKHOLM • ATHENS • TOKYO

Original hardcover edition published in 1979
by Mills & Boon Limited

ISBN 0-373-02482-7

Harlequin edition published June 1982

To

AUDREY

with many pleasant memories
of our days in Madrid

The house was full of packed suitcases; people were going away. Catherine Royce surveyed the little pile on the polished floor of the hall with mixed feelings as she drew on her gloves, realising that the scene was not new to her. Over the years her parents had departed for distant corners of the earth with amazing regularity, leaving her in the charge of one relative or another when she had been too young to go with them and sending her off to boarding-school when she was older. Later, when her schooldays were over, they had remained in England just long enough to see her safely installed at the college of her choice before they had hastened off to India, and now they were bound for America on a lecture tour which would last for a year.

A whole year, Catherine thought, full of new experiences for them all because now she, too, was going away.

Her mother came swiftly down the curving staircase from the floor above, a tall woman in her late forties with a thin intelligent face and fine brown hair which she wore coiled closely round her head.

'Have you everything you'll need, my dear?' she asked in the practical tone she used when she was organising her husband's journeys to far-away places. 'Passport, immunisation certificate, your letter of introduction, any medication you may need, a book for the journey?'

'Everything, Mother. You needn't worry, I'm fully equipped for the direst emergency!' Catherine reached up to kiss the sallow cheek burned by constant exposure to drying winds and sun. 'I might be just a little bit nervous about meeting these people, but that will probably sort itself out when I do. The agency assured me that they were a good family—"well-respected" was the phrase they used

—and would give me a pleasant home.' She held her breath for a moment. 'Quite apart from teaching English to a young Spanish *señorita*, I'll be brushing up my own Spanish and gaining an impeccable accent.'

'You're really quite sure you want to go?' There was a suggestion of doubt in Nancy Royce's eyes as she asked the question, although she could not understand any daughter of hers not wanting to travel abroad. 'You really ought to spread your wings a little and make some practical use of your gift for languages.'

Catherine turned towards the staircase, furious with herself for wanting to cry, for wanting to stay here in the only home she knew.

'Is Father ready?' she asked to cover a desperate sort of loneliness, a desire for belonging. 'I really ought to have ordered a taxi.'

A tall, spare man in a grey suit made his appearance on the floor above, coming to the baluster rail to look down at them.

'Ah, there you are!' he observed. 'All ready to go?'

'Ready and waiting.'

The Professor came slowly down the stairs. He had been over forty when his only child had been born, too old to adapt to a baby in the house, and Catherine had always thought of him as vaguely kind, but she loved him dearly. He had talked to her like a grown-up person for as long as she could remember, encouraging her in her school work, passing on the knowledge he felt would be useful to her, but he had never been able to cope in an emergency, his thoughts being fully taken up by his profession. It had been left to her mother, who was more practical in every way, to make all the necessary decisions, and it was Nancy Royce who had advised her daughter to make the most of her fluent Spanish and seek a position abroad.

She kissed her daughter on each cheek as the Professor reached the hall.

'Do your best, my dear,' she admonished. 'A first job is always exciting, but it can also be demanding. I'm sorry I can't come with you to the airport,' she added, checking the pile of suitcases on the floor, 'but we leave ourselves at three o'clock and there are still a score of last-minute jobs to attend to. You understand?'

'Perfectly!' Catherine kissed her in return. 'I'll write just as soon as I get there,' she added. 'I have your New York address.'

On the way to the airport her father sat beside her in a protracted silence for a long time before he produced a package from the capacious inside pocket of his shabby overcoat.

'It's a book,' he explained almost apologetically. 'I thought you might like to have it. It was written by an old friend of mine and it's about Spain. Spanish history, really.' He put the package on her knee, patting it gently. 'I think it will interest you and give you a truer insight into the Spanish character.'

Their fingers touched for a moment over the book.

'Thank you,' Catherine said. 'I'll treasure it.'

He looked vaguely uncomfortable.

'We'll meet you in a year's time,' he said. 'Meanwhile, Cathy——'

'Yes?'

'If anything should happen, if you're ever in any difficulty, go to the Embassy. I've given you the address on the Fernando el Santo in Madrid, just in case.'

'What could go wrong?' Catherine asked as he parked the car. 'I shall be doing a job to the best of my ability and if I don't succeed and am asked to go I shall look for another one.'

'Best to come back to England, in that case,' he advised, 'but I don't think there's any fear of you falling down on the job.'

'That's because you're my father!' She gave his arm a tight squeeze. 'There are a hundred reasons why I might fall flat on my face!'

He smiled his disbelief.

'I was thinking more of the people you might meet,' he

confessed. 'I find people difficult, but I hope you're more like your mother and can deal with them.'

'I'm like you—a dreamer,' she wanted to say, but the words would not come. Perhaps, she thought, I should steel myself to be my mother's daughter, after all.

When the big jet lifted off at the end of the runway she turned the book he had given her over in her hands, but she did not open it until they were south of the great barrier of the Pyrenees and she was looking down on the broad Iberian peninsula for the first time. It was then that her father's parting gift seemed truly significant, a guide which might help her to understand the people she was about to meet and the land in which they lived.

It was a slim volume, easy to read and beautifully illustrated, a brief record of Spain's colourful history 'written in blood and gold'. When her concentration strayed she looked down on the scene beneath her, on Castile, the land of castles, wondering what she would find there. Dreaming, she allowed her thoughts to wander until the book slipped from her fingers to be retrieved by the smiling air hostess who had welcomed her aboard.

'Your first visit?' the girl asked. 'You'll love Madrid. I'm always happy to be on this route.'

She handed back the book as it had fallen, open at one of the illustrations which graced the central pages, and Catherine found herself gazing down at a man on horseback. *El Conquistador.* She read the caption beneath the picture with a sense of shock because horse and rider had seemed suddenly to come alive. They had grown out of the page to become even larger than life, yet the armour they wore placed them securely in the past. It was a statue in bronze, the man's face finely chiselled to suggest strength of character and purpose, his firm hand clenched on the shaft of the tall lance he carried, yet there was a hint of cruelty about the mouth and a suggested arrogance in the proud carriage of the head which she did not like. These were the men who had gone out to conquer a whole new world, men of ambition and a fierce, inherited pride to whom ruthlessness was a way of life, yet she tried to imagine a look of compassion as well as purpose in the forward-gazing eyes. No doubt the statue was one of Jaime I of Aragon, the *conquistador* king, or one of his many conquering knights.

Abruptly she closed the book, thrusting it deeply into the pocket of her travelling satchel because the man on the bronze horse had disturbed her with a look and because they were no more than five minutes away from Madrid.

The sprawling capital of Spain rose like a mirage from the vast tablelands which surrounded it, an oasis of colour in the lonely stretches of slaked sand and granite mountains lying beneath her. It was not what she had expected; not from the air, anyway.

'Fasten your seatbelts, please.'

The hostess came along the aisle, looking from side to side to see if her request had been complied with, and then, almost imperceptibly, they had touched down. It had been an uneventful flight except for the fact that the portrait of a man on a bronze horse had disturbed Catherine for no reason that she could possibly understand.

Dismissing the thought, she followed her fellow-travellers to the exit, proffered her passport for inspection, and found herself walking down the length of the main hall wondering how she would identify the person who had come to meet her. Apart from the fact that she would be picked up at Barajas and should display the agency card prominently in her hand she had no way of telling who might be waiting for her, but she supposed it would be someone from the Madroza household, probably a chauffeur with the family car to take her luggage.

Then she saw him. It was the man on the bronze horse whose proud face and concentrated gaze had disconcerted her as he had sprung to life from the printed page. He wore a plain grey suit and white shirt, with a striped silk tie in grey and maroon, nothing to connect him with a knight or a *conquistador* king, but there was the same look in his eyes, the same autocratic turn of the head as he surveyed her fellow-travellers one by one. The proud scrutiny passed over her as he walked on, but somehow Catherine knew that he had come to meet her. She made a small, brief movement with the agency card, hoping that he would see, but for a moment the arrogant back was turned and she was still unrecognised.

No doubt she had been wrong. She drew a sigh of relief, aware that she had been deeply shaken by the encounter, and looked about her for a more prosaic figure in the uniform of a chauffeur.

'Miss Royce?' The man was standing beside her looking down at the agency card from his substantial height. 'Forgive me if I passed you by originally, but I was looking for someone quite different. Someone much older,' he added deliberately.

'I'm sorry,' she found herself saying. 'I had no idea I should have been in my dotage.'

Her sardonic rejoinder seemed to glance off him.

'You have other luggage?' he asked, glancing at her travelling satchel. 'We must go immediately to pick it up.'

His English was impeccable, with only the slightest hint of an accent in his deep voice, but he was frowning. In one way or another she seemed to have displeased him. She hesitated, conscious of the slow pounding of her heart.

'You are——?'

'Jaime de Berceo Madroza,' he introduced himself, inclining his dark head in what might have been a bow. 'My grandmother wrote to your London agency some time ago and we had your answer last month, but I do not think you mentioned your age. However, it is essential that we have a tutor for my niece immediately.'

'But you're disappointed that I'm not middle-aged.'

A faint smile touched his lips.

'I am not your employer,' he returned briefly. 'Your age —or lack of it—must be a question for my grandmother to settle in her own way. You seem to have the qualifications she asked for, and perhaps age was not stipulated. Have you your luggage receipt and I will collect it for you?'

He held out his hand in a commanding gesture which she had almost expected and she gave him the luggage slip to go in search of her suitcases. In a few minutes he had returned with them on a trolley pushed by a willing porter, although there had been very few in evidence when she got off the plane. A man like Jaime de Berceo Madroza, she reflected drily, would be able to conjure them out of thin air.

She followed the tall, distinguished-looking figure out to a waiting car. It was long and sleek and beautiful, suggestive of wealth in an unobtrusive way, a worthy vehicle, no doubt, for the man who strode by her side, and he held the door open for her with the courtesy she should have expected.

'We have not far to go,' he informed her politely. 'But perhaps you have been in Madrid before?'

Catherine shook her head.

'I haven't even been to Spain before,' she confessed. 'This is a first time for me for everything. I've never taught English before, I'm afraid, but I have an adequate knowledge of Spanish, which was all the agency asked for. I believe I was the only suitable person available.'

Except for my age, she thought, when he did not answer her immediately. He seemed to be concentrating on the rapid flow of traffic which sped towards the capital, although he drove with ease. Catherine stole a quick glance at the chiselled profile silhouetted against the sudden green of trees as they glided along: the high forehead surmounted by thick black hair, the finely-pencilled brows drawn over the commanding dark eyes, the long, aquiline nose and hard mouth all culminating in a strong chin which gave the face its true character. A man of iron, used to command, who would brook no disobedience from anyone who served him just as he would hold himself on a tight rein where his own responsibilities were concerned. The fact that he was here, in an expensive limousine, driving rapidly towards the heart of one of the liveliest capitals in the world, seemed incongruous in the extreme, completely out of character, in fact, when she could see him so clearly pictured on a bronze horse with a lance in his gauntleted hand and all the hard purpose of a *conquistador* king in his eyes. He should have been far from Madrid making his mark on the wider world, riding over vast estates, but perhaps that was no more than her over-active imagination at work. In her first position in a strange land she would have to be more practical in her outlook and less of a day-dreamer in order to make a success of what she had undertaken.

As they drove into the heart of the city a quick excitement stirred in her veins, for this was all that she had expected, and more. Wide thoroughfares and elegant, tree-lined *plazas* opened out in all directions, with new and ancient buildings lining their sides and an air of spaciousness everywhere she looked.

'A great deal of Madrid is being rebuilt to make way for the future,' her companion explained. 'My grandmother deplores the fact that venerable old buildings have been pulled down to widen the boulevards for the increasing traffic, but what is the use of trolley-tracks when the trolley-cars themselves are no longer viable? The relics of the past are rapidly being swept away, but City Hall has been wise enough to consider the traditional Castilian values of reserve and austerity, too. They hope to strike a happy medium between yesterday and tomorrow, and I think that they will succeed.'

'It looks a lovely city,' Catherine agreed, taking in the broad panorama of elegant buildings and busy thoroughfares with shining eyes. 'I know I shall be happy here.'

It was a foolish remark to make, she realised, because the man by her side would be no more concerned with her personal happiness than her real employer would be.

'Your grandmother?' she asked. 'Does she live in the city?'

'At its very heart. She would never wish to live anywhere else,' he said. 'She is a true *Madrileña* who still enjoys her own tempo of living, although she moves out of the city like everyone else for two months in the summer when the heat becomes unbearable. She is, you see, a very practical person, ready to compromise when she can do nothing much about a situation which gets out of hand.'

Was that some kind of warning? Catherine glanced at Jaime de Berceo Madroza and wondered, knowing that he would be too polite to show his true feelings to a stranger. The age-old Spanish tradition of courtesy and hospitality would be rigorously observed, no matter what he thought about their present situation, but she could not forget the swift frown which had momentarily darkened his brow when they had met for the first time.

Driving into the heart of the city, they came to a wide *plaza* where high fountains sparkled in the sunshine and the unmistakable likenesses of Don Quixote and his faithful Sancho rode in deathless stone. Side streets flanked by large mansions originally built for the nobility, which were now either museums or public offices, led to a quiet residential area where the brick façades of the houses were steeped in sunshine and mellowed by time.

'We are almost at our destination,' Don Jaime told her. 'My grandmother will be waiting for you.'

In spite of her resolution not to be intimidated in any way, Catherine was suddenly nervous of this second meeting with a member of the Madroza family, for it seemed that his formidable grandmother who would have the final say about her suitability for the position she had come to fill was no mere figurehead but an active participant in the affairs of the family in general.

They drew up before a stout mahogany door in a brick wall over which could be seen the tops of high trees set, no doubt, in an ancient garden. The street itself was so quiet as to seem almost deserted, yet a few minutes ago they had been driving along the busy Avenida de José Antonio, the Great White Way stretching through the heart of Madrid. Her companion got out from behind the steering-wheel to open the door on her side of the car.

'I will see to your luggage,' he said.

'Thank you.'

Formality hedged them round, yet she had the disconcerting feeling of being carefully observed. Before they reached it the door in the wall was opened and an ancient retainer saluted them.

'You will see that the *señorita*'s luggage is taken to her room, Lucio,' Don Jaime commanded. 'I will look after the car myself.'

The old man nodded, offering Catherine a tentative smile.

'*Buenas tardes!*' he greeted her. '*Yo el sigo.*'

When he had collected her two suitcases he followed them across the enclosed garden to the house itself, a tall, three-storeyed edifice with small, wrought-iron balconies at the windows on the upper floors and a grilled door which stood hospitably open to bid them welcome. In the hall beyond an old lady in a dark silk dress stood leaning on an ivory-handled stick, her slender, delicate-looking hand gripping it closely. Although obviously depending upon its support, her back was as straight as her grandson's and her large black eyes equally clear. They scrutinised Catherine with frank curiosity, taking in the cut of the plain blue suit she wore and the sensible low-heeled shoes, finally coming to rest on her face and the silken, red-gold cap of well-brushed hair which surrounded it.

'*Abuela*, this is Miss Royce,' Don Jaime said, turning to leave them, but his grandmother held up a detaining hand.

'You will lead her to her room, Jaime, and then I will expect you in the *salón* to take tea with us in the English manner,' she commanded. 'No doubt your routine has been disturbed by the services I have asked of you, but this is an important matter as far as Teresa is concerned.' She was still gazing at Catherine. 'Indeed, I am surprised, but we will go into that later.'

Don Jaime nodded abruptly, while Catherine felt that she had been weighed in some sort of delicate balance and found wanting.

'Your grandmother seems to disapprove of me,' she said

as Don Jaime led the way to a flight of marble stairs. 'What is it this time, or is it still my youth?'

He looked round at her with a faint smile in his eyes.

'You must not judge my grandmother as quickly as you have judged me, *señorita*,' he said. 'She would not come to any swift conclusion about you. She will wait till you have shown her your true worth. She will give you the benefit of the doubt, as you so succinctly say in your own country.'

'But you wouldn't?' she challenged. 'You are prepared to judge me untried!'

'That would not be so if I were employing you myself, but in that case I might have been more explicit in my demands,' he pointed out.

'Of course,' she said, feeling at a disadvantage. 'How old is your niece, Don Jaime?'

'Sixteen. A great age, you may be sure! Teresa is full of confidence, you will find, and quite certain of the way she wants to go, but that might not be entirely her own fault. Small Spanish girls are brought up from babyhood to believe themselves the centre of the universe. They are told from birth that they are *guapa*, as you know, and so they are spoilt.'

'While little Spanish boys are encouraged to be *macho*!' she pointed out drily. 'You can't criticise one while you applaud the other.'

'Encouraging a boy to be masculine is not quite the same,' he said dismissively, 'but you will judge Teresa for yourself, I dare say. She has gone for a music lesson, by the way, if that is where she really is.'

His voice had hardened on the final words, as if he did not trust his effervescent niece who had been encouraged from infancy to believe that she was incredibly beautiful.

'I hope I can understand Teresa,' Catherine said involuntarily. 'Already I feel sorry for her.'

'You needn't be. She is a very fortunate young lady, although she does not acknowledge the fact. She is also very headstrong,' he added, 'and prone to go off at a tangent when she feels "imprisoned".'

Catherine paused on the landing.

'Surely you don't mean me to act as her jailer!' she exclaimed. 'It's something I would hate to do.'

'Not at all.' His voice was as cold as ice. 'I am her legal guardian, as you may have guessed, and I am greatly concerned about her welfare.'

'Have you ever thought of slackening the rein—giving her a little more headway? I know she's young to be kicking over the traces at sixteen, but it's happening all the time nowadays,' Catherine pointed out.   '

He turned to look at her.

'How old are you, Miss Royce?' he asked without attempting to answer her impulsive question.

'Twenty-two.'

'And have you ever "kicked over the traces", as you put it?'

'I—never really needed to. You see, I was trusted to be sensible, even when I was very young. My parents were abroad a great deal, and I owed it to the aunt who looked after me to conform to her ideas of normality.'

'Ah,' he said, pausing before one of two massive doors set in an archway at the far end of the upper hall. 'That is quite different!'

He opened the door, ushering her into a pleasant room full of sunlight with windows opening on to a small balcony overlooking the side garden and a narrow lane beyond the wall. The room itself was full of fine old Spanish furniture in the style of a century ago, family heirlooms which had been handed down from one generation to the next and greatly treasured. A heavily-carved wardrobe took up much of one wall, while a four-poster bed stood against another, flanked by little tables skirted in pale blue brocade. On the third wall, between the two long casements, stood an exquisite writing-table with a brocade-covered chair placed in front of it, ready for her use, while a dressing-table and a black, carved chest stood on either side of a communicating door leading into a large, tiled bathroom.

'Thank you,' she said again. 'It all looks—very comfortable.'

'And very sedate!'

A young, dark-haired girl had entered the room behind them, frankly amused by what she had heard of their conversation. Catherine knew that this must be Teresa even before they were formally introduced, and if insisting since babyhood that she was *guapa* had been meant to enhance her confidence it had certainly succeeded. Catherine thought that she had never seen anyone so lovely as Teresa in that moment as she stood beside the door with a world of merriment in her eyes. Added to their dark, magnetic beauty was a flawless, apricot-tinted skin and blue-black hair and small, delicate hands and feet which made her look like a pretty, animated doll. She drew in a deep breath of appreciation as their eyes met.

'I can't quite believe it!' she exclaimed in her accented English. 'You really are young and with it!' She looked up at her uncle, a mischievous smile curving her red lips. 'What do you think of her, Jaime?' she demanded. 'Isn't she quite fantastic, or do you disapprove of her as firmly as you did of Madame Mauriac?'

'Madame Mauriac taught you to speak French without an accent, therefore she did what was expected of her,' Don Jaime observed. 'We can only hope that Miss Royce will be equally successful with your English.'

'Which is atrocious!' Teresa acknowledged without due concern. 'Perhaps it is because I have no true desire to learn,' she suggested.

'You will try,' her uncle decided with a firmness which put any doubt in its proper place.

Teresa continued to study Catherine as he left the room.

'You're not at all what I expected,' she said, at last. 'Not what anyone expected, for that matter. When I think about it we could have lots of fun together while we are allowed to stay here in Madrid. I hope it will be for another week or two,' she ran on excitedly, 'but in that respect we must wait for Don Jaime's decision. He is the *árbitro* of our fate, both here and at Soria. You will see!' Her vivid little face took on a sullen expression which marred its beauty and the dark eyes were suddenly alight with passion. 'I am old enough to do as I wish without everyone directing me this way or that,' she declared with fierce intensity. 'Spanish girls are now emancipated; they go everywhere on their own and take advantage of life. They are no longer protected by eagle-eyed *dueñas* who do not wish them to enjoy themselves. They are free!'

'I'm sure you are permitted to please yourself, up to a point,' said Catherine, aware of conflict but unwilling to take sides. 'Your family must have your ultimate welfare at heart.'

'But not my happiness!' Teresa declared with an obstinate stamp of her foot. 'They know that I wish to dance and they say that there is still time. Time for what? To drink in culture and take a university degree so that I will be "equipped" for the future. What does that mean, I ask you? To be a great dancer would be of equal importance, don't you think?' She rushed on before Catherine could form an opinion. 'It is all *their* way and not mine, and then they wonder why I should rebel. I have everything I can possibly desire, both here and at Soria,' she mocked, 'and that must be the end of any argument!'

Pushed by family pride and hedged round by tradition, Teresa had come to a stubborn halt, digging in her heels like the little mules of the Spanish countryside, her ears laid flat against her dainty head. Catherine suppressed the smile which rose to her lips, knowing how serious Teresa was.

'We all feel that way occasionally,' she sympathised. 'We long to spread our wings and fly away at one time or another, but it is not always best to do it in a spirit of rebellion. I'm sure, when the right time comes, your grandmother and Don Jaime will agree to set you free.'

'You do not know Jaime!' Teresa cried. 'He is as hard as a rock. What rock is it that is harder than any other?'

'Granite,' Catherine supplied much too quickly.

'Well, that is as hard as he is! You will see,' Teresa declared. 'He can also influence Grandmother, which is more than anyone else can do.'

Catherine felt that Teresa was only telling her what she already knew. Don Jaime de Berceo Madroza was the undoubted power behind his grandmother's throne. The old lady might be the distinguished head of the family, but her grandson had the final say. She wondered about Teresa's parents, about the mother and father who had not been mentioned so far, but Don Jaime had described himself as Teresa's guardian, so perhaps they were both dead.

She began to have a certain amount of sympathy for this lonely girl brought up at second-hand, so to speak, although she knew that it was dangerous to form such firm opinions on such a short acquaintance.

'I'll help you to unpack,' Teresa offered, dismissing the young Spanish girl who was hovering in the doorway. 'You may go, Conchita,' she said with an autocratic wave of her hand vaguely reminiscent of her uncle. 'Tell the Marquesa we will not be long.'

The girl hesitated, her dark eyes apprehensive.

'It is my work, *señorita*,' she objected in Spanish.

Teresa stamped an impatient foot.

'Do as I say!' she admonished. 'It will save time if I help Miss Royce. You are so slow!'

The girl retreated, shamefaced by the hasty criticism, and Teresa laughed.

'There you are! I am quite heartless, as you can see, but I *wished* to help you and look at all your lovely clothes!'

'I think you may be disappointed,' Catherine smiled, prepared to humour her, 'but shouldn't we go down to the *salón* immediately and not keep the Marquesa waiting?' She decided that the difference in their respective titles must mean that the old lady was Don Jaime de Berceo Madroza's maternal grandmother. 'I'm finding everything a little difficult just now,' she confessed. 'And I don't want to antagonise anyone.'

'Don't be afraid,' Teresa replied chirpily. 'You will already have antagonised Jaime, anyway. He does not like women ever since one of them decided to betray him a long time ago.'

A cold little shiver ran through Catherine at the knowledge. So that was the reason for Don Jaime's apparent dislike of her! It was nothing personal, as she had originally believed, but a deep-seated dislike—hatred, perhaps—of all women, as Teresa had implied.

'Even so,' she found herself saying, 'I mustn't start off on the wrong foot. The Marquesa said she would be waiting in the *salón* and we really ought to go.'

'You must want to wash first,' Teresa suggested, her inquisitive gaze still lingering on the suitcases. 'I will wait for you.'

It took Catherine less than ten minutes to wash and tidy her hair, but when she returned from the bathroom Teresa had gone. Unpredictable, she thought, like most girls of her age, but peculiarly likeable even on such short acquaintance!

Would they get on together, she wondered as she descended the wide staircase, or would Teresa come to regard her as an irritating watchdog employed to check on her every movement while she endeavoured to teach her the finer points of the English language? Determined not to act as Teresa's jailer under any circumstances, she opened the *salón* door.

Old customs were scrupulously observed in the Marquesa's household and Catherine found that her 'English tea' was strictly a Spanish affair. It was served by a male retainer with a *muchacha* hovering in the background ready to run for more hot water or extra cakes, and it was a meal in itself. The average Spanish woman's addiction to pastries would no doubt spoil Teresa's figure in time unless, if she really wanted to be a dancer, she could bring an inflexible will to bear on her present capacity for the lethal sweetmeats. She ate heartily, enjoying them to the last crumb, while the Marquesa looked on indulgently.

Don Jaime stood in the background skilfully balancing his teacup and a plate in one hand, but eating little. He had been deep in conversation with his grandmother when Catherine had entered the room, but their exchange of confidences had ceased abruptly as soon as she appeared. He drew forward a chair for her.

'Sit down, Miss Royce,' he said briefly. 'We have been discussing the future.'

Catherine glanced in Teresa's direction to find her frowning into her teacup.

'I asked the agency for an older woman,' the Marquesa said, looking at Catherine, 'but no matter. We will see what you can do.'

'I think you had a copy of my references,' Catherine responded formally. 'If not, I have the originals with me; also my college certificates. I understand your language, but naturally I hope to benefit by living in a Spanish household. That was part of my reason for coming.'

'And the other part?' Don Jaime asked coldly.

She turned to face him.

'My parents have travelled a great deal for as long as I can remember,' she explained, looking directly into his hostile eyes. 'My father is a university professor who does a lot of research and they are not often at home. Now they have gone on a lecture tour of America which will keep them away from London for the best part of a year.'

'I see,' he said as if he had discovered her true reason for taking the job. 'It would inconvenience you a great deal to return to England at this stage.'

Catherine swallowed the hard lump in her throat which must have been disappointment, turning to look at the Marquesa.

'If you have come to the conclusion that I am unsuitable,' she said firmly, 'of course I must go.'

'We do not make decisions as swiftly as that,' the old lady answered. 'When you have finished your tea you must go and supervise your unpacking. I take it you brought all your luggage from the airport?'

Catherine hesitated.

'I sent some books overland. I thought they might prove useful when I came to read with Teresa in English.'

'That was very thoughtful of you,' the Marquesa agreed. 'Jaime will see that they are picked up as soon as they arrive.'

'Please let me do that for myself,' Catherine begged. 'Don Jaime must have other things to do.'

'It is a service we perform for our guests,' the Marquesa declared, looking keenly at her grandson. 'Jaime will be glad to oblige.'

It was difficult to accept the old lady's assurance, because Catherine felt quite sure that Don Jaime would have sent her packing back to London if he had any say in the matter, but apparently the final decision would be his grandmother's.

She did her own unpacking in the end because Teresa had disappeared and the dismissed Conchita was now keeping her distance. The capacious wardrobe which stretched most of the way along one wall of her bedroom was more than adequate for her needs, and soon her skirts and dresses were carefully hung up and the blouses and sweaters she had brought installed in the row of glass-fronted drawers in the end section of the wardrobe.

What to do now? The final meal of the day in a Spanish household was rarely taken before ten, and it was not quite six o'clock. Catherine crossed to her windows to look out, wondering if Teresa might come in search of her, but although she stood looking down into the enclosed garden for another ten minutes she was not disturbed. There was no sign of life in the *patio* beneath her windows nor in the garden beyond where a riot of flowers blazed beneath the trees in the bright sunlight. There would be no harm in her going down, she felt, to enjoy the last of the sun and sit for a while on one of the narrow stone benches under the trees.

When she reached the hall she saw that the *salón* door was open and for a moment she hesitated.

'It is unfortunate that she is so young, so very near Teresa's own age.'

The Marquesa's voice floated out to her, and suddenly she was standing stiffly in the centre of the hall waiting for the reply to the old lady's remark.

'More than unfortunate,' Don Jaime returned. 'I feel that it might even prove disastrous, but we have no time to change our minds now.'

He was standing just inside the *salón* door, and Catherine knew that she had to escape. Otherwise, she felt that they would be involved in an angry exchange which would do nothing to resolve the situation and could prove completely embarrassing. She had already made her offer to return to England immediately, an offer which the Marquesa had rejected, saying that she must be given a fair trial and, after all, she was in the old lady's employment and not her grandson's. She decided to ignore Don Jaime, although that might be very hard to do. Cautiously she turned back towards the staircase.

'Ah, Miss Royce!' he said, coming to the open door. 'Were you about to join us?'

'No.' She swung round to meet his mocking smile. 'I was looking for Teresa. I thought she might be in the garden.'

He did not believe her; the mockery was still in his eyes, accusing her of eavesdropping.

'I did hear what you said,' she told him bluntly, an angry colour rising into her cheeks, 'but I can't see that it makes much difference. You are not my employer, and I will do my best for the Marquesa. That way I feel justified in staying here for the time being.'

'It is as you wish,' he acknowledged briefly, 'and as my grandmother desires. She has decided to try you out and I will look after the books you have so thoughtfully consigned by rail for your future use.' He looked at her long and searchingly. 'You do know, of course, that you will not be living in Madrid for any length of time. This is not Teresa's home.'

'Oh! I thought——'

'It was no more than an accommodation address till we settled the problem of her further education,' he went on to explain as distantly as before. 'Teresa has been long enough in Madrid.'

Catherine had to keep reminding herself that he was Teresa's guardian, yet he had allowed her to believe that the Marquesa was her true employer.

'My grandmother goes south, to Andalusia, for the summer months and Teresa and I return to Soria. My work is there, not in Madrid.'

'I had no idea.' A fleeting memory of the equestrian statue pictured in her father's book flashed across her mind, the man on horseback with the look of conquest in his eyes, a man so like Don Jaime de Berceo Madroza as to seem uncannily the same. Yet she had never seen him seated on a horse. On the contrary, he still wore the immaculate light grey suit which made him look every inch the conventional Spanish business man, and his thick dark hair was sleeked back closely against his head. No helmet, no plume, no lance grasped firmly in those shapely hands! She smiled faintly at the thought. 'Of course I understood we would be staying in Madrid,' she added carefully, 'but it really doesn't matter where we live. I thought Teresa might be going to university here.'

'Eventually, if we can dissuade her from taking up a career as a dancer,' he said.

So he did know about Teresa's secret ambition and firmly disapproved of it on principle.

'Perhaps that is where her real talent lies,' she suggested impulsively.

'If I thought so we would consider it more seriously,' he decided. 'Teresa, at the moment, doesn't know what she wants, Miss Royce. She is young and volatile and sometimes very foolish when she imagines that she has the bit between her teeth. It is nothing new in our family, I assure you, but while I am responsible for her welfare I must be sure that she conforms to a reasonable code. My grandmother thinks that she should be encouraged to go on with her formal education until she is quite sure what she wants to do.'

'And you don't really consider sixteen to be the age of discretion?'

'In your country it may be so, but in Spain it is not so long ago that emancipation was never spoken about. Girls did as they were told, and although I don't believe in them living in seclusion until they are old enough to be married, they had very little experience of freedom. Sixteen is too young an age to loosen the parental grip altogether. You can see that I take my responsibilities fairly seriously,' he added, 'although you may not agree with my methods.'

She was forced to smile.

'I have no right to criticise,' she conceded.

'So we are in agreement in that respect, at least.' He led the way towards the *patio* door. 'I dare say you will find Teresa outside at this hour. She likes to walk the dog.'

Teresa came in by the door in the wall as Catherine turned along the garden path. She was leading a small dog which seemed to be a cross between a poodle and a dachshund and she looked dishevelled, although there was very little wind.

'I've been to the park,' she explained. 'Ferdi doesn't get enough exercise shut up in the house most of the day, and besides'—she lowered her voice—'I meet people I can really talk to. If my family had their way I would only meet the people they know—their sons and daughters— and they are mostly stuffy intellectuals who talk of nothing but politics or art or what they will do when it becomes too hot to stay in Madrid.'

Some sort of chemistry was developing between them. Catherine, who felt half sorry for Teresa and wished to understand her point of view, could already feel it, although she knew that it would be dangerous to encourage the younger girl's rebellion against the present situation or even to advise her until she actually asked for some sort of direction.

'I thought you liked Madrid,' she said instead.

'Sometimes I wish I could stay here all the time,' Teresa confessed, letting Ferdi off the lead, 'but even if I do come back to university I would only be here during the term. Even that would be better than it is now,' she mused, swinging round to face Catherine in the fading light.' You know what's going to happen, of course? We are to be packed off to the *hacienda* to vegetate there all summer. I have been too long in Madrid for everyone's liking!'

Something pathetic about the impassioned declaration touched Catherine in a sensitive spot.

'Tell me about the *hacienda*,' she said.

'Oh, it's beautiful, of course, and the climate is perfect —neither too hot nor too cold, even in winter—but it is so isolated you just wouldn't believe!' Teresa's face clouded. 'There is nothing for me to do all day except ride or swim or go visiting on the neighbouring estates and obey my stepmother because she is devastated by my father's death. That was an accident. There were ugly rumours, but I don't believe Jaime had anything to do with it. I think my father had a quarrel with someone else.'

Catherine drew back aghast at what she had just heard.

'I wouldn't repeat that unless you're absolutely sure,' she cautioned. 'Ugly rumours are hard to suppress. I thought you were—quite fond of your uncle.'

'In an odd sort of a way,' Teresa agreed, sitting down on one of the stone benches to continue the conversation. 'You see, he has been more like my brother. He was ten years my father's younger—junior, I mean—and now he is the proud owner of Soria, which was something he coveted, I suppose.'

A chill ran through Catherine as she sat on the edge of the bench, as if a cold little wind had blown against her heart, but she had no intention of getting too deeply involved with this amazing family, no intention of taking sides.

'Surely you're wrong,' she said, aware that her volatile young pupil might be prone to exaggeration. 'Don Jaime doesn't look the kind of person who would covet his brother's inheritance.'

'Perhaps not,' Teresa allowed, 'but you have yet to learn how ruthless he can be. I said that I did not believe the rumours and I think that my stepmother would like to marry him, but I do not say so because I am not supposed to know about such things.' She laughed, her white teeth flashing against her apricot-tinted skin. 'They imagine that I am still a child and I have been sent to Madrid to absorb a little culture, but I am tired of the Prado and all the Goyas and Velázquez and the tapestries well-brought-up Spanish girls embroidered in the past!' Her lips parted excitedly. 'I can show you another Madrid, Cathy—the one I love—full of music and romance. I will go one day to the University at Casa de Campo and it will all be mine!'

'And worth waiting for,' Catherine suggested.

Teresa considered her with thoughtful eyes.

'Tomorrow I will show you,' she promised. 'We have not long before we leave for the *hacienda*.'

CHAPTER TWO

THE meal they shared in the long dining-room was quite elaborate. As the sun went down behind the distant Guadarramas they had gathered in the small *salón* while Don Jaime poured them each a glass of sherry, but no toast had been proposed either to the future or the past. It was a nightly routine, Catherine supposed, when he raised his own glass to the light and saluted his grandmother with a brief smile. The Marquesa returned his smile, as if words were quite unnecessary between them, and they all went in to dinner.

The old lady sat at the head of the table in a high-backed chair and he occupied the place at the far end after seeing Catherine and Teresa safely seated in their respective chairs. Above them a magnificent chandelier hung from the painted ceiling, shedding its yellow light on the highly-polished wood and on the glittering silver and crystal which adorned each place-setting, and the old retainer who had brought their tea served them with Conchita's help. Don Jaime rose to carve the joint of meat at the massive sideboard which occupied most of the wall behind his chair, and it was almost midnight before they rose to take their coffee in the adjoining room. When the little silver carriage clock on the mantelpiece struck half-past twelve Catherine followed Teresa up the staircase to their respective rooms.

'I am not to chatter,' Teresa said when they reached her own door, 'because you must be tired after your journey. *Buenas noches, señorita!*' she added with a small, mocking laugh. '*Usted habla español muy bien!*'

'And you will do well with your English in time,' Catherine responded. 'It'll be fun learning together!'

In the morning Teresa was waiting for her at the breakfast table, looking excited.

'I am to take you to the Prado this morning, but we will not remain there all the time,' she said. 'Jaime has promised to take us to lunch,' she added quickly when Catherine was about to protest. 'It is quite in order, you see. He will join us in the museum and we will eat in a restaurant of his choice.'

Catherine was surprised, but perhaps the Marquesa had made the request and he would not refuse her. She felt sure that he could not *want* to take them out for a meal.

The old lady's breakfast was carried up to her room each morning at nine o'clock, and before they left for the museum they went in to pay their respects to her. She looked like a queen sitting there in the great four-poster bed with its heavy canopy of intricately-carved wood and the richly-brocaded curtains shielding her from any possible draught. The room itself was cluttered with the accumulated treasures of a lifetime, photographs and souvenirs from her travels, precious bric-à-brac and small pieces of silver, heavy combs from her Andalusian girlhood and a beautiful collection of ivory and silk fans which was displayed in a bow-fronted cabinet between the windows and on the high chimneypiece on the opposite wall.

'You will enjoy our city, Miss Royce,' she said as Catherine stood beside the bed. 'Especially the Prado. It is many years since I have been there, but one day I must go again just to sit and absorb the beauty of the true masters. You know our famous Goyas, of course—the *majas* and his clever portraits—but there are many other artists of note also on display. Do not try to see everything in one morning,' she warned, 'for that would be impossible. Teresa has been many times, but does not yet truly appreciate what she sees.'

'I think that if I had decided to be a painter instead of a dancer it would have been all right with my family,' Teresa said with a pout as they went down the stairs. 'Shall we take a taxi?' she added brightly. 'Or would you rather walk?'

'A taxi might be quicker if we are to see as much as possible before one o'clock,' Catherine decided, thinking that Don Jaime must not be kept waiting.

Sitting close up at the window, she gave her full attention to the beauty of the Spanish capital. Wide, tree-lined avenues spread in every direction, flanked by gardens and magnificent buildings, many of them originally built for the old aristocracy in marble and polished stone. Where change had been inevitable it had been made with the past in mind, and there were flowers everywhere and cool stone benches under the trees.

At the end of the Calle Mayor they turned into the Calle de Alcalà with the Plaza de Cibeles fountain directly ahead of them.

'We are nearly there,' Teresa informed her, gathering up her satchel and silk headscarf.

Catherine was spellbound, gazing at the magnificent centrepiece of the square with the chariot-mounted daughter of Uranus rising out of the water drawn by two stone lions. It was the most arresting group she had ever seen, the Greek goddess dominating even the cathedral-like Palacio de Comunicaciones on the opposite corner, and even here there were trees and benches and a shady promenade where the *Madrileños* could take their ease.

The taxi driver set them down at the side entrance to the museum and from there onwards Teresa was in charge.

'I know every crumby inch of the way,' she declared in practised slang, 'but it is something we must do if we want the remainder of the day to ourselves. The Vegas have asked us to eat with them later on, but we can make our excuses and come away early. I have a plan, you see, to show you more of Madrid.'

'One thing at a time!' Catherine laughed, following her into the great rooms where they wandered for an hour before they sat down to rest.

Time after time Catherine had found herself confronted by the portraits of men so like Don Jaime as to be almost his painted likeness, although all of them wore the clothes of a bygone age. Stern, dark eyes gazed back at her from under domed helmet and velvet cap, the aquiline nose and long, determined chin predominating wherever she looked, features handed down through generations of Spaniards to the present day. All of them had been men of great strength and vision, the conquerors who had gone out to claim a new world for their own. Painted as Velázquez had seen them, they were magnificent, and their blood still flowed in the veins of Jaime de Berceo Madroza.

They filed through the rooms containing the paintings of Goya's 'black period', when he was already deaf, turning into the longer galleries which Teresa said she liked better. Before one of the larger groups of a royal family she paused.

'This one always fascinates me,' she declared. 'It says so much. It is Charles IV and his queen, María Luisa, and her boy-friend, Godoy. Horrible, isn't he? Like a bull. How could she have loved anyone so gross?' She examined the royal group for a moment longer. 'My stepmother had a lover before my father died,' she announced almost casually. 'Nobody thinks I know, but I do!'

Catherine looked round at her in surprise.

'Surely that's something you shouldn't repeat,' she said uncomfortably.

'Why not, since it is true?'

'Where is she now?' Catherine asked, knowing even before Teresa supplied the answer.

'At Soria—where else? She is determined to live there until Jaime asks her to marry him. Then she will once again be the undisputed mistress of the *hacienda*.'

Catherine drew in a sharp breath.

'Surely that's your uncle's affair,' she suggested. 'If he's in love with her he'll want to marry her.'

'Jaime isn't in love with anyone—yet. He has still to get over his first disappointment with women,' Teresa declared, sounding much too old for her years. 'Would you like to hear about it?'

A faint colour stained Catherine's cheeks.

'I've listened to enough family gossip for one morning,' she declared more hastily than she realised. 'It doesn't concern me, Teresa.'

'It might,' Teresa suggested slowly, 'if you were to fall in love with Jaime.'

'That would be ridiculous!' The colour in Catherine's cheeks deepened. 'Anyway, here he comes! Please don't repeat what you've just said,' she added hastily.

Don Jaime strode towards them.

'Have you had enough culture for one day?' he asked, glancing at the pictured group they had been studying. 'A cruel portrait,' he observed, 'but it was a degenerate age.' He looked at his watch to check the time, dismissing the royal husband and his faithless wife with a shrug. 'Where would you like to eat?'

'Surprise us,' Teresa suggested. 'You know all the best places.'

They went in search of his parked car and he drove them along the Castellana to a secluded restaurant on the top floor of one of the higher buildings where Catherine could enjoy a panoramic view of the city while they ate, and somehow he seemed more mellow as he ordered their sherries, naming points of interest for her benefit as he stood at her shoulder to point them out.

Turning suddenly, she caught an amused twinkle in Teresa's eyes, but for once she refrained from her usual sly observation and kept silent.

'What do you intend to do with the remainder of the afternoon?' Jaime asked when he had ordered for them. 'Go shopping?'

'I have to be measured for a pair of shoes,' Teresa explained carefully, 'and I will collect my shirts from Antonio.'

'And spend a great deal of money in the boutiques,' he suggested good-humouredly. 'I'm sorry I can't collect you later in the day as I have an appointment in Toledo, but I believe you are going on to the Vegas for an evening meal.'

Teresa nodded somewhat hastily.

'That is what has been arranged,' she agreed.

Jaime looked pointedly at Catherine.

'I will leave her in your care, Miss Royce,' he said formally. 'I hope you will enjoy the rest of the day.'

'I've enjoyed it very much up till now,' Catherine told him. 'Thank you for a pleasant lunch.'

Teresa was laughing as they turned away.

'You and Jaime are so formal!' she declared. 'Perhaps it is because he does not trust you.'

'Why should you think such a thing?' Catherine protested. 'I'm trying to do my job to the best of my ability, and you could help enormously by not being so facetious.'

'That's an interesting word,' Teresa declared. 'Can you please tell me what it means?'

'Broadly speaking, it means "waggish", which in turn means jesting. You don't mean what you say half the time, especially about Don Jaime.'

'Oh, but I do! He can be stern and quite heartless when he feels justified, and at Soria, you will discover, his word is law.'

'Supposing he decides that I shouldn't go to the *hacienda*, after all,' Catherine suggested in an odd sort of panic. 'It's quite on the cards, you know.'

'H'mm! Yes, I suppose it is, but I think you will go, all the same. The Marquesa will send you because she thinks you might be good for Soria.'

'Where do you want to shop?' Catherine asked because she could find nothing to say to Teresa's final declaration.

It was now well after three o'clock and they walked briskly through the crowded streets which were coming to life again after the *siesta* hour. On Velàzquez Teresa was measured for her handmade shoes and they spent more time on the Alcalà until suddenly they realised that it was six o'clock. The coffee houses and pastry-shops were now full of women chattering over their *merienda*, but Teresa seemed disinclined to stop even for a quick glass of chocolate and a cake.

'We will call on the Vegas early,' she suggested, a flush of excitement staining her cheeks, 'and then we can make our excuses. I want to take you *tascas*-hopping. It's lots of fun and something you really ought to do before we leave Madrid.'

'What will the Marquesa say?' Catherine asked diffidently. 'Or Don Jaime?'

'Oh, Cathy!' Teresa protested. 'How will they know? We will be home before midnight if we go early enough, but you really must see our busy *mesones*. They are a kind of tavern—terribly respectable, you understand—and most of them are in the old part of the city which is the real Madrid.'

Catherine hesitated.

'If you're quite sure,' she said doubtfully. 'I feel that I'm more or less in charge at the moment.'

'As if you could be when you know so little of Madrid!' Teresa laughed. 'You will be glad to get away from the Vegas, I assure you!'

They took a taxi to a rather drab-looking edifice in a side-street leading off the Calle de Segovia which was the home of the Vegas, where they were entertained by an elderly lady and her two nephews, whom Teresa obviously disliked. Catherine thought them pleasant enough, but dull, and was almost glad when Teresa rose to go. She made her pretty excuses to the *señora*, dismissed the two polite young men with a brief smile, and shepherded Catherine out on to the pavement in the shortest possible time. They heard a clock strike nine as they walked briskly in the direction of the Plaza Mayor.

'You needn't look so worried,' Teresa assured her. 'Nothing is going to happen to us. You are a good *dueña*, are you not?'

'I'm out of my depth,' Catherine admitted. 'Teresa, I think we should go back.' She looked about her at the maze of narrow, cobbled streets with their closely-shuttered windows and barricaded shops. 'We can come some other time—with Don Jaime, perhaps.'

'He would not come here, unless on a very special occasion,' Teresa said, 'but he would not object to you seeing the real Madrid, especially when we are so soon to go away.'

It seemed a reasonable enough argument, and Catherine followed her across the wide *plaza* to an archway and down a flight of stone steps to where a dozen small taverns spilled their light and gaiety on to the adjacent pavements. Most of them were already full of people searching for a table, but Teresa seemed to know her way about. She selected the nearest side café where she ordered shrimps, mushrooms and *tortilla*, together with two glasses of *carta blanca* which they drank standing at the counter.

'We haven't time for any more *tascas*,' she decided when they had finished. 'It's rather a pity because you can spend a whole evening just hopping from one café to another and eating as much as you like.' She turned along a darkened side-street where a mellow glow led them to the window of a secluded restaurant.

'You'll love this,' she said, plunging in at the door.

It was at this point that Catherine had the strongest misgivings. But the restaurant looked eminently respectable, a tall, narrow house of many floors reached by a single staircase on which departing and arriving guests seemed to be inextricably mixed. Groups of tourists rubbed shoulders with the local *Madrileños*, laughing and talking as they filed between the crowded tables, determined to make this an evening to be remembered, and Teresa nodded to several acquaintances as they passed.

Finally they were installed at a small table for two in a corner. Teresa's eyes were alight with a new intensity as she gazed about her and an American lady at the next table said in a loud voice: 'My, but she sure is cute!'

'Cute' was hardly the word to describe Teresa in that moment. She was completely transformed. A band of minstrels dressed in the garb of Philip II was serenading the diners for money instead of the traditional love, but they were immensely talented young men and truly colourful in their velvet knee-breeches and tunics with the large, slashed sleeves of the period and their capes festooned with satin favours in all the colours of the spectrum. One, in a voice which echoed to the rafters, was singing a love-song.

'They are university students,' Teresa whispered. 'They form groups to play and sing in the restaurants. Isn't it romantic!'

'O, my beloved,' sang the vocalist, while the guitars and a single violin played the accompaniment. Then, when the applause had subsided, the guitars came into their own. Sobbing out in the sudden hush which had fallen on the noisy room, the music started on a plaintive note, a few soft chords gently plucked from the delicate strings, but soon it was rising on a wave of anguish, a lover pleading in the night for trust and understanding.

Catherine sat rigidly in her seat, the music vibrating on every sensitive nerve as she listened, her hands clasped tightly in her lap, until she became aware of the man standing in the doorway at the head of the stairs.

Don Jaime had come in search of them, his face dark with anger as their eyes met.

'It's Jaime!' Teresa exclaimed in a half-whisper. 'He must have returned early from Toledo.'

Don Jaime made his way purposefully between the tables, drawing the eyes of most of the American women as he passed and striding between the minstrels as if he would sweep them from his path, and none of the anger had left his face when he finally confronted them.

'How did you know where to find us?' Teresa asked. 'We have just come in.'

Ignoring both question and observation, he sat down in the vacant chair opposite his niece.

'I presume you have already ordered your meal,' he said in a tight voice, 'and you may wait for it, but I intend to take you straight home after your first course.'

'Oh, Jaime!' Teresa wailed. 'You spoil everything! Catherine wanted to see the night life and it was *so* dull at the

Vegas'. You say yourself that they are only half alive!'

'That may be so,' he agreed, 'but you were supposed to be there and you were not. When I arrived to take you home—you had gone.' He was holding his temper in check with an effort. 'If Miss Royce was so keen to sample our night life you should have mentioned the fact when I took you to lunch and it could have been arranged for some other time.'

'But there is so little time!' Teresa pouted. 'Botín's is most respectable and Catherine should get some "atmosphere" instead of always dining in a top-class restaurant.'

Don Jaime turned to Catherine for the first time. He was evidently not going to make a scene in a public place. He was too well bred for that.

'I'm sorry you found our rendezvous on the Castellana so dull,' he remarked, 'but no doubt this evening will make amends.' He glanced beyond her at the minstrels in their velvet doublets while their impassioned music rang like a knell in Catherine's ears. 'Botín's has always been a colourful tourist trap, but the food is excellent, I believe.'

Catherine, who had been enjoying the atmosphere in the picturesque seventeenth-century building as well as the talented performance of the students, was suddenly angry.

'I thanked you for a very pleasant lunch,' she reminded him, 'and I really meant what I said, but this is different. I didn't see any reason why Teresa and I shouldn't have come here for a meal, but if I was wrong I'm sorry. It seems a shame not to take advantage of so much innocent pleasure, but no doubt I should have been more—discreet.'

'It is Teresa who should have known better,' he said briefly. 'The point is that she came here without permission while you were supposed to be somewhere else. The Vegas are very old friends of the family and we do not wish to offend them. Such things are not done in Spain, even yet,' he added as a waiter approached with their order of roast sucking pig on ancient earthenware platters which had been burned almost black with constant use.

Catherine's appetite had gone, but she forced herself to

eat under his eagle eye while he orderd a *fino* and drank it
while he waited.

The minstrel students came to stand beside them, playing softly, but most of the romance had gone from their
performance for Catherine, at least. She could no longer
respond to the gentle words, and the sighing guitars were
almost more than she could bear.

Teresa braved out the situation with what seemed to be
a total disregard of his anger.

'Jaime, you must admit that it is all wonderfully romantic,' she sighed, looking across the table at the violinist
with wide soulful eyes. 'You play the guitar yourself: why
do you think this is not the same?'

'Possibly because it is no more than a gimmick,' he returned as the serenading group moved away. 'They do it
solely for the money they can make.'

'I think you are wrong,' Teresa declared. 'They sing with
all their hearts and we respond to the music, not to them.'

He looked amused.

'So long as that is the case,' he said, 'who am I to reprimand you!'

Had his anger evaporated so easily, Catherine wondered, or was he only holding it in check till they left the
restaurant and he could tell them what he really thought?
The evening had been spoiled, as much for herself as for
Teresa, although Teresa was quick to find another delight.

'This little pig is delicious!' She dug into the succulent
flesh. 'Why don't you try some, Jaime? Now that you are
here we can stay much longer.'

'You are expected home before midnight,' he reminded
her. 'You are supposed to be visiting privately.'

The dark eyes under their thick fringe of black lashes
were suddenly lifted to his.

'Does that mean you are going to keep our secret?' she
demanded. '*Gracias*, Jaime!' she rushed on before he could
make his decision one way or the other. 'It is very
kind of you, and I will obey you in future. I will do anything you wish!'

'It would be nice if you meant what you said on the spur of the moment,' he returned drily, but some of the anger had already gone out of his eyes and he settled more comfortably into his chair to enjoy another *fino* while they disposed of their sucking pigs.

'Catherine can't finish hers!' Teresa pointed out a few minutes later. 'She has no appetite now, perhaps because you were so angry with her.'

'I was angry with you both,' he said, 'but since no harm has come from your foolish venture, we will try to forget it.'

Catherine could not forget his anger, however, that initial flash of impatience which had darkened his eyes, hardening his whole face even as she watched, and somehow she knew that Teresa's disobedience was only part of the reason. There was also her own part in their adventure to consider, and it seemed reasonable enough for him to consider her completely irresponsible. He had been at little pains to hide his feelings when they had first met and now she seemed to be confirming them.

By quarter to twelve they were driving in the stream of traffic along the Calle de Bailén and just before midnight they were home. A light was burning in the Marquesa's room on the second floor and it seemed that they were expected to go there to report on their 'happy evening'.

It amazed Catherine to see how skilfully Teresa managed to evade the truth. Her animated description of their visit to the Vega household suggested that nothing could have been more congenial than the *señora*'s company, and the fact that Don Jaime had 'collected' them to bring them home seemed the most natural sequel at the end of their busy day. She rushed on to talk about the Castellana luncheon party, which she was able to do without avoiding her uncle's disdainful gaze.

'I'm glad Miss Royce enjoyed herself,' the Marquesa observed drily, 'even although I'm afraid that Isabella de Vega is a little dull,' and suddenly Catherine knew that she was not deceived. That penetrating gaze, so reminiscent of Don

Jaime, had seen straight through Teresa's wiles, but she had evidently decided not to pursue the subject at that time of night.

In the morning, perhaps? Catherine's heart was beating fast as she followed the younger girl from the room.

'Teresa, you should have told the truth and accepted the consequences,' she pointed out. 'Even now, I am not at all sure that your uncle has forgiven us.'

'We will know quite soon,' said Teresa. 'Perhaps tomorrow.'

In the morning the preparations for their departure were all too evident. Don Jaime had gone off to the Rastro early to make some important purchases from one of the *galerías* before they closed at two o'clock, and Conchita had been instructed to begin Teresa's packing.

'We are going so soon!' Teresa wailed. 'It is all because we are no longer to be trusted. I told you about Jaime, did I not? He has a will of iron once he has made up his mind.'

The Marquesa said very little. Soon she would be on her own way to Andalusia to avoid the summer heat, but there was still no question of Catherine being dismissed. When Teresa finally challenged her, however, she admitted that their departure for Soria was only a matter of hours away.

'If Jaime can reserve seats you will fly out in two days' time,' she explained.

'Two days!' Teresa gasped. 'But that is impossible. I have all my clothes to collect, my shoes and the new dresses from Antonio.'

'They will be sent on to you,' the Marquesa assured her. 'I will see to it myself, do not fear.' She looked across the room at Catherine. 'It will not take you very long to repack your suitcases, Miss Royce. I think you will be good for Soria,' she added with an enigmatic smile. 'Anyway, we shall see! You must not let Lucía dominate you, although you will obey her, of course. That is understood. Until Jaime decides to marry she will be mistress at Soria and she will not allow you to forget the fact, I think.'

'Lucía is my *madrastra*,' Teresa informed her as they left the room together. 'You will hate her, as I do. My father married her after my mother died, but they were not happy together. All she wanted was the position as his wife so that she could do as she pleased. I do not believe my father really loved her, because she is not beautiful, as my mother was, but she has a will of iron. When she marries Don Jaime she will send me away, but I do not care. I will return to Madrid and stay here with the Marquesa.'

It was the following day before Catherine came face to face with Don Jaime again and by that time she had done most of her re-packing.

'I'm sorry I have not been able to trace your books,' he apologised, 'but I will make the necessary arrangements to have them sent on to Soria. You will not be without them for long.'

'I seem to be giving you a great deal of unnecessary trouble,' she found herself saying. 'If I tender my resignation will it help?'

He looked down at her from his considerable height, frankly surprised by the suggestion, although he had done nothing to encourage her in her job.

'You cannot do that now,' he informed her. 'It would be utterly irresponsible. I have made a promise to my sister-in-law to bring Teresa back with a tutor'—he refrained from using the word 'suitable'—'and there is no time to change our arrangements now. You will be ready to leave tomorrow, if you please. The flight goes out at midday, so you have little time to squander.'

On dubious adventures? Her anger stained her cheeks, but she was determined not to let him see how easily he could upset her.

'Where do we fly to?' she asked, wondering why they could not make the journey by road since he had a powerful limousine at his disposal.

'To Tenerife,' he said. 'Surely Teresa has told you that is where we live?'

'Tenerife?' Catherine repeated incredulously. 'No, I had

no idea we would be going so far. You have all referred to Soria as "the *hacienda*", but I imagined it might be some- where in Andalusia since your grandmother is preparing to go there for the summer. I never guessed that we would be leaving Spain.'

'You are going to an island that is still part of my country,' he pointed out. 'I do not expect you to fall in love with Tenerife straight away—Teresa will colour your opinion too darkly for that—but it is a beautiful island, one of the loveliest in the world, in fact.'

'The "Lost Atlantis"!' Catherine murmured. 'Or is that too fanciful a thought, *señor*? I've read about your island, but I've never been there. This will be something new for me, although it was unexpected.'

'I hope that Soria will not disappoint you,' he said to her further surprise. 'My sister-in-law has lived there since my brother's death and, of course, it is also Teresa's home. I see no reason to alter these arrangements at the moment. We are a family of which I am now the head. When my brother was alive I also lived on the *hacienda*, but in a smaller house by myself, but that is changed. Teresa will tell you that Soria is a prison, but I try to make life as pleasant as possible for her. She has everything she needs, within reason, but unfortunately she has a chip on her shoulder—a stepmother chip!'

He smiled, and she was amazed at the difference it made to his dark countenance, erasing the lines which she had believed to be permanently etched between his brows.

'We might be able to help her over that particular hurdle,' she suggested. 'Teresa is very young for her age in some respects.'

'I thought you young for your age when we first met.' The disconcerting confession was so unlike him as to seem completely out of character. 'But perhaps I am a bad judge of women.'

'I've done nothing to convince you otherwise since I came,' Catherine admitted, 'but I really didn't see anything wrong about going to Botín's without permission the other night. It wasn't exactly polite to leave the Vegas' so early. I realise that now and I'm very sorry.'

'You have already apologised,' he told her in the autocratic tone which she found so disconcerting. 'We will say no more about it. You must see that I have to keep Teresa on a fairly tight rein because she is so impetuous and often foolish, but I really do understand how she feels.'

It was an admission which she had not expected him to make and it melted the ice a little. In some ways he was quite human.

'Perhaps we can work something out once we get to Soria,' she suggested.

He looked doubtful.

'Perhaps we can try,' he said.

The following morning they took their leave of the Marquesa, although she did not wish them goodbye. '*Hasta la vista!*' she said. 'We will meet again.'

They drove to the airport in plenty of time for their flight, their luggage piled in the capacious boot of the car while Catherine sat beside a pouting Teresa in the back seat.

'We could have stayed for one week more,' she complained. 'This has been Lucía's doing. She cannot bear Jaime to be away from Soria for too long.'

Catherine thought that it had much more to do with their own disobedience, but refrained from saying so because Teresa was in no mood for a reasonable argument. If Lucía had indeed sent for Jaime the fact that he had come running seemed also out of character, although it was difficult to judge if love had a hand in it.

She had become increasingly curious about Lucía, the woman who had married one Berceo Madroza for the power it would give her and who now wanted to marry his brother for a reason best known to herself. Love? Of course, it could be love. Lucía might be madly in love with Don Jaime and she already had one claim on his allegiance. She was his brother's widow and in the Spanish household she was, therefore, his responsibility. When he had spoken about her he had accepted the fact.

The flight was shorter than she expected. They went out
over the sea, low enough to watch the Iberian coastline
fading away behind them, and by the time a meal had
been served they were well above the Atlantic. Seated beside Teresa, Catherine felt a new excitement stirring in her
veins, the lure of far-away places which her father had
known for so long. She wondered if she was a wanderer at
heart or did she really believe that there must be a place
somewhere for her to put down roots?

She read a little, glancing at Don Jaime in the seat on
the far side of the aisle from time to time, but he was busy
with a thick sheaf of correspondence which he had taken
out of his briefcase at the beginning of the flight, suggesting
that he had no need for conversation to while away the
time. Teresa gazed moodily out of her porthole between
bouts of thumbing through the magazines she had bought
at Barajas, but presently she sat bolt upright in her seat
to stare out towards the horizon.

'You'll get your first view of the island in a moment or
two,' she announced. 'I suppose it's something you
shouldn't miss, although Jaime thinks it's more dramatic to
see from a ship. I'll tell you when to look.' She remained
poised on the edge of her seat, peering through the porthole at the cloudless blue sky beyond the wing-tip and the
blue sea beneath. 'El Teide is our resident mountain and
you can see him a long way off, like a lost pyramid sitting
on the horizon. Look, there he is now, taking shape! Today
he has his little cap on his head, but most of the time he
is quite clear!'

Catherine could just make out a vague, conical shape,
the ghost of a mountain peak riding the waves like a distant ship. It was so far away as to be scarcely discernible
at first, but she watched in silence as it came nearer, slowly
emerging from the mists of distance with a white cloud-
cap on its head. Teresa had sounded excited when she had
spoken about El Teide, yet only a few hours ago she had
called Soria a prison. Was it only the *hacienda* she disliked so much?

'He governs all our lives, that great mountain,' Teresa was saying. 'He is always there, so close sometimes that you believe he has come stealthily in the night to hear what you say. But he can also be a distant giant, wrapped in his mantle of cloud till he is almost hidden away. The labourers at Soria are afraid of El Teide; they are superstitious of his power.'

Catherine's gaze still lingered on the distant peak, but suddenly she looked up to find Don Jaime standing beside her.

'What do you think of our resident giant?' he asked. 'The first time you see him will remain for a long time in your memory. When you live in his shadow you will come to know him better.'

His dark eyes were fixed on the approaching mountain and she knew instinctively that this was his land, the place where he had put down roots which went deep beneath the surface, the place where he wanted to be. If he had only come to Soria because of his brother's untimely death that did not matter. He *was* Soria now and that was enough. She could not believe that the mark of Cain was on his brow, as Teresa had hinted, although she had quickly denied the gossip to affirm her belief in him.

'The Fortunate Isles!' she mused, looking down on the smudge of sun-kissed islands lying just ahead of them. 'I've always thought it a lovely description.'

'It is a name you have to discover for yourself,' he said. 'Tourists come here and go away, but they rarely know the islands as they really are. Of course they are fortunate when the sun shines most of the time and the temperature rarely falls below sixty degrees along the coast, but they have a hidden face which you have to come to terms with, sooner or later. Once you have done that you can find happiness.'

'Have you always lived here?' she asked.

He nodded.

'We are a fourth generation at Soria. The estate was granted to one of my ancestors for services to Spain when your Admiral Nelson was defeated at Santa Cruz. That was a long time ago,' he smiled, 'but you will see that my roots go very deep.'

Catherine gazed down at the islands lying beneath them now in a sea of incredible blue. There were seven of them in all, a little world on their own washed by the vast Atlantic swell but so near to the coast of North Africa as almost to be lying in its mysterious shadow. For a moment, as she looked, a little chill wind seemed to blow across her heart, yet they were compounded of sunshine and light, each with a character of its own.

'Gran Canaria is the loveliest of them all,' Teresa declared as they fastened their seatbelts, 'but we seldom go there. Jaime's world is on Tenerife, at Soria, and that will be your world, too, while you remain with us.'

They began to lose height on their approach to Tenerife, with the giant, El Teide, watching from the mountain fastness of Las Cañadas, which was his home, but as they circled the white port lying at the edge of the sea Catherine realised that they would touch down farther inland on a high plateau on the northern end of the island.

'La Laguna was a natural landing strip,' Jaime told her. 'It serves both sides of the island equally well.'

What she could see of their landfall was curiously disappointing at first. Tenerife, even when it was bathed in dazzling sunshine, looked dark and forbidding, with deep black valleys piercing the landscape and harsh gullies biting deep into the mountainsides. Then, as they drew nearer, she could see the lush green of trees and crops ripening in the sun and clusters of little white houses clinging to the mountainsides, and the face of the island was suddenly fair.

Set high on a small amphitheatre among the mountains, La Laguna was a gem. Catherine had never seen so many flowers blooming so lavishly all at once and she could well believe that their perfume could be wafted across the water to passing ships in the more leisurely days of sail to gain the Canaries the romantic title of the Fortunate Isles. She thought about the ancient Guanche who had inhabited these lands for a thousand years, living as though their little islands were the whole world and nothing beyond the sea mattered to them.

'Well, we're here!' Teresa said in a flat tone.

Almost imperceptibly they had touched down on the wide apron in front of the main reception area, and Catherine gathered her hand-luggage together while Don Jaime took down her white woollen coat from the overhead rack.

'You're not going to need this,' he said, 'once we get away from the mountains.'

When they reached the reception lounge he appeared to be searching for a familiar face among the many Spaniards waiting for friends and relations as they came off the Madrid plane.

'There's Ramón!' Teresa cried, dashing forward to embrace a tall young Spaniard who had just come in through the revolving doors.

'My younger brother,' Don Jaime explained. 'I did not think he would come, but it is certainly pleasant to be met by one of the family.'

Teresa was approaching with Ramón in tow and Catherine found herself looking into a pair of dark eyes which were frankly appraising. Ramón de Berceo Madroza, unlike his older brother, was prepared to accept her on sight, possibly because they were of an age and because he had always had an eye for a pretty girl. He, too, had obviously expected her to be much older, and his frank acceptance of her was a sure sign of his surprise and delight.

'*Bienvenida, señorita!*' He bowed over her hand, a gesture Don Jaime had never permitted himself. 'You are happy to be in Tenerife?'

Catherine hesitated, but only for the split second it took to glance in his brother's direction. Don Jaime was frowning.

'Very happy, *señor*,' she answered firmly, 'although it doesn't really matter where I work.'

'You will enjoy the *hacienda* once you have got used to

us,' Ramón assured her, 'and soon all our errors with your difficult English language will be swept away!'

His tone had been gently teasing, his dark eyes still admiring.

'If you are ready, Ramón, we will make a move,' his brother said drily. 'We have a long journey before us.'

A fleeting spark of resentment kindled in the younger man's eyes, but it died almost immediately as Ramón helped load their accumulated luggage on to a trolley which a porter trundled out to the large black car waiting for them in the car-park.

Catherine drew in a deep breath of the keen mountain air as she followed Teresa, looking around her at the massed blooms in the immaculate flowerbeds and beyond them to the dark green of a pine forest which clothed the nearer hills. The island rose steeply from the sea and up here on the plateau it was more like Scotland than the sub-tropical island she had expected, but soon they were in the car and driving westward towards the coast. The road which had climbed two thousand feet up to the plateau from Santa Cruz de Tenerife now twisted downwards in a series of hairpin bends which afforded them breathtaking views of the other side of the island, of an ochre-coloured coastline fringed by a line of white breakers and backed by a second sea of green banana fronds swaying gently in the cool breeze which had followed them down from the mountains.

'It's beautiful—really beautiful!' she exclaimed involuntarily. 'I had no idea it would be like this.'

'Wait till you see Soria,' Ramón promised, sitting beside her in the back seat. 'You will fall in love with that, too.'

Don Jaime was driving, with a silent Teresa sitting beside him, but he drew the car up at a suitable passing-bay to let her admire the glorious panorama beneath them. Tropical vegetation had now taken over from the darker line of the forest, and red and violet bougainvillea grew everywhere, cascading over ochre walls and the little houses clustered by the wayside, drooping flamboyantly

from a balcony on a lonely farm and sometimes trespassing
on to the road itself. Palms had replaced the sombre firs of
the mountainsides and an avenue of tall eucalyptus
stretched for miles, the tiny leaves, like silver coins, spinning in the wind. Far away and always present, the giant
conical peak of El Teide rose against the sky, his white
cloud-cap doffed in salute.

'Thank you,' said Catherine when Don Jaime started the
car again. 'It was good of you to stop.'

'It is a view to remember,' he said. 'Down there is Puerta
de la Cruz, which was once the fruit port for the valley, but
now it is mainly a tourist centre. Soria is more remote,' he
added on what was surely a note of warning.

'Will we stop at Orotava?' Teresa asked hopefully. 'You
could give us tea at the English Club, Jaime.'

'Why not?' her uncle agreed. 'It is not far out of our way.'

Orotava was a sub-tropical paradise, with masses of
bougainvillea everywhere and little pink and white geraniums growing wild in the ditches beside the road. They
approached it along an avenue of eucalyptus trees which
seemed to shimmer in the afternoon heat, but presently
they entered the shaded grounds of the Club and were
immediately found a table under an arcade of vines where
tea was brought to them on a silver tray, with scones and
cakes and plenty of guava jelly.

The unexpected break in their journey gave Catherine
more time to think about their destination. It was obvious
that Soria was well off the beaten track, a small kingdom
on its own where Don Jaime de Berceo Madroza ruled
supreme. In thinking of the *hacienda* she automatically
wondered about Doña Lucía, who was Teresa's stepmother
and temporary mistress of Soria. What would she be like?
Kind or condescending or even frankly hostile? It was impossible to say.

'Don Jaime, of all people!'

The cool, English voice broke in on her reflections and
she looked up to find a tall, fair-haired girl of about her

own age standing by Don Jaime's side. He rose immediately to offer her a seat.

'I'm playing croquet,' she announced, laying her mallet
aside, 'but I have just time to be introduced.' She was looking at Catherine. 'You're from England,' she suggested. 'Are
you on your way to the *hacienda*?' An underlying doubt
had tinged her voice for a moment and then she laughed.
'Don't tell me you're Teresa's tutoress!'

'Miss Royce—Miss Alexandra Bonnington,' Don Jaime
introduced them formally. 'Alex is quite a character around
Orotava,' he added. 'She paints!'

'Which sounds as if I commit all the deadly sins at one
go!' Alex Bonnington laughed. 'But I can assure you that
I do it for a living. Otherwise, I couldn't afford to stay here.
Jaime only sees me on the rare occasions when we're both
able to relax.' She looked at Catherine with a deepening
interest. 'I hope you'll be able to come to Orotava now
and then, Miss Royce,' she said. 'We have an excellent lib-
rary at the Club and there are plenty of English people
around if you feel in need of a chinwag in your own language. Hullo, Teresa!' She turned to the younger girl with
a faint smile. 'Are you still the little rebel without a cause?'

'Not without a cause,' Teresa answered with more dignity than Catherine would have suspected. 'I know what
I want to do in the end.'

Alex had practically ignored Ramón, giving him no more
than the briefest of nods.

'Will you take some tea with us?' Don Jaime asked. 'We
were just about to begin.'

'I'd love to, but I was on my way to make up a four-
some,' said Alex, picking up her mallet. 'Why not drop in
and see me one day?' she invited as she shook hands with
them for the second time. 'Do you paint, Miss Royce?'

'I'm afraid not, though I've often longed to try,' Catherine confessed.

Alex Bonnington considered her for a moment in silence.

'You may need something to do in your spare time,' she
suggested. 'Teresa will bring you to see if you can.'

Again there was the underlying doubt in her voice which Catherine was quick to detect.

' 'Bye!' said Alex. 'Till we meet again.'

They met swiftly and unexpectedly half an hour later in the ladies' cloakroom.

'I've cut my hand,' Alex explained, holding her wrist under the cold water tap in one of the basins. 'Terribly silly of me, really. I just don't know how I did it. I broke a tumbler while we were having some squash to drink and groped under a bench for the pieces. I bleed like a pig,' she ran on, 'so don't get alarmed. It's not at all serious, I assure you.'

'Please let me help, all the same,' Catherine offered. 'If we had a bandage——'

'Teresa will go for one,' Alex suggested. 'Ask at the office, Teresa, there's a dear, sweet girl!'

While they waited Alex allowed the water to trickle slowly over her wrist.

'How are you going to cope?' she asked.

'With Teresa?' Catherine hesitated. 'I think we'll see eye to eye sooner or later. Teresa isn't very pliable just now, as you may have guessed, and she wants to be a dancer more than anything else, but she has plenty of time to change her mind, although I don't think it's exactly my task to help her to the right decision. I'm here mainly to teach her to speak English.'

'I wasn't thinking of Teresa,' Alex said carefully. 'I was considering the whole set-up at Soria. You haven't met Lucía yet, I gather, so I feel that I should warn you to be on your guard. Lucía will be your enemy, and I don't envy you. She can't possibly be expecting anyone like you, anyone so young. I don't mean to sound too alarming,' she added quickly, noting the rising colour in Catherine's cheeks, 'and of course, this is only a job as far as you're concerned.'

'I would wish my work to be satisfactory to Don Jaime and Doña Lucía equally,' Catherine said a little stiffly.

Alex laughed, although not unkindly.

'You must be quite starry-eyed,' she declared, 'but you have yet to meet Lucía.'

Teresa returned with the necessary bandage, leaving Catherine to tie it while she looked on.

'Splendid!' Alex commented, surveying her wrist with satisfaction. 'I won't bleed to death, after all! 'Bye, once again. I'm sure Jaime will be wondering what's happened to you.'

Don Jaime was standing beside the parked car, glancing at his watch. He seemed impatient, and Catherine was surprised to find how far the sun had travelled down the sky.

'Jaime will want to reach Soria before nightfall,' Teresa explained. 'He will know that my stepmother expects us before dark.'

Catherine offered their apologies.

'Miss Bonnington had a slight accident,' she explained. 'She cut her wrist and I bandaged it up for her.'

'Something's always happening to Alex,' Ramón observed. 'Is she badly hurt?'

'No, not at all. It wasn't a very deep cut, but it bled a lot.'

They got into the car, the men in front this time, with Ramón driving. Don Jaime had not offered to occupy the back seat.

Retracing their way along the same road, they branched right to travel high above the sea, and in the rapidly-fading light Catherine could just make out the black volcanic line of the shore with white waves, like lace, breaking along it and the calm stretch of dark water beyond which seemed to stretch to infinity. Above them, dominating the whole island, stood the Pico de Teide, withdrawn now into his mountain fastness to sleep away the coming night.

The road they followed stretched for miles, always high above the sea, with a small township here and there clinging to the hillside. It all seemed so far removed from the busy world of Orotava and its guardian port and the brash new hotels which had sprung up to cope with an increasing tourist trade. This was the real Tenerife in all its desolate splendour, scarred by black rivers of calcined lava which had flowed from Teide's last eruption and dark with mystery.

Abruptly Ramón turned the car inland, climbing a little way before they began to drop down into a hidden valley where all the lush vegetation of the north was renewed. The sea was behind them now and densely wooded hills closed them in, but the land on either side of the road was intensely cultivated. Fields of bananas stood motionless in the still air, while figs and vines clothed the foothills in terrace after terrace, irrigated by a semi-circular dam at the top. This wide cultivated strip stretched as far as the eye could see until they came to a high wall running beside the road, and here Ramón slackened speed and Catherine's heart began to pound because she knew that they had reached Soria, at last.

At a wide, arched doorway in the wall they pulled up, and almost immediately the door was opened by a small, swarthy youth who saluted them as they passed through. Ramón turned the car along a brick-paved road bordered by a hundred flamboyant plants and flowers whose scent rose headily into the evening air, assailing their nostrils as they drove along. One perfume seemed to dominate, and Catherine turned to Teresa to ask what it was.

'Stephanotis,' Teresa replied indifferently. 'It is everywhere.'

The house itself lay in a little hollow sheltered by a group of palms, its *adobe* walls gleaming pinkly in the pale evening light, an old house built many years ago in the Moorish style and added to periodically as the family grew. Planned originally round an inner courtyard, it had expanded on either side, with broad arches leading from one section to the next and a central fountain which leapt high into the air to splash back into its ancient stone basin filled with waterlilies.

The main door of the house stood wide open, but nobody waited to greet them.

Don Jaime got out of the car and crossed the *patio*, while Teresa and Ramón took a little longer to follow him. There was no joy in this homecoming for Teresa, apparently, and Ramón put their luggage down on the flags and drove away. Don Jaime turned back at the door.

'Leave them to Alfredo,' he commanded as Teresa lingered beside the suitcases. 'He will attend to them.'

Inside the house a great commotion had begun, with several female voices rising in unison somewhere at the rear of the hall, an excited chatter of servants as they realised that the master of the house had returned. Two of them appeared at an inner door, the older one smiling broadly, the younger painfully shy in the presence of a stranger.

'Eugénie! Sisa!' he greeted them. 'This is Miss Royce from England. You will attend to her, Sisa, while she remains here.'

The younger girl seemed pleased, although she did not step forward immediately, sheltering behind the older servant's maturity. She was small and plump, with a mane of sleek, straight hair flowing around her shoulders and a broad face out of which glowed a pair of large, dark eyes.

'*Sí, sí!*' she agreed eagerly, rushing off to help with the luggage.

Catherine glanced about her at the great hall with its beautifully tiled floor gleaming in the light of a magnificent wrought-iron lantern which hung from a central beam, and then, suddenly, she was aware of being watched.

A long gallery ran round three sides of the hall, reached by a magnificent branched staircase, and at the head of the stairs a woman stood waiting. In the shadows above them she looked extraordinarily tall in her long-skirted black dress which was wholly devoid of ornamentation, and the fact that her wealth of black hair was worn high and braided to form a coronet about her shapely head did nothing to detract from the illusion as she came slowly down the stairs towards them.

Lucía, Catherine thought. This was the present and, perhaps, the future mistress of Soria. It was then that she noticed the ruby. A large, unmounted stone, it hung by a slender chain round Lucía's neck, burning against her bare flesh like fire as the light from the lantern leaped in its many facets, bringing them to glowing life. It was utterly magnificent, yet peculiarly evil in some curious, inexplicable way which she could not understand, a thing of beauty which could also destroy.

'Lucía,' said Jaime, 'this is Teresa's new tutoress, Miss Royce.'

Catherine met the dark eyes above the glowing ruby, conscious of the scarcely controlled fury in their depths.

'How is this so?' Lucía demanded, addressing her brother-in-law in Spanish. 'It is not as we wished. You know that, Jaime! It is some mischief of that old woman, your grandmother. She is a viper! She is determined to have a finger in every pie!'

The smile faded from Don Jaime's face.

'Miss Royce may be younger than we expected, Lucía,' he said quietly, 'but she is also competent to teach Teresa, and this we must accept. A mistake has been made, but that is impossible to change now. Please see that she is welcomed to Soria in a reasonable manner and comfortably housed.' He drew himself up to his full, commanding height. 'Our hospitality must not be impaired by the fact that she is not what we expected.'

Lucía turned on the bottom stair.

'Come this way,' she said in halting English, as if she was almost reluctant to use the language which Don Jaime wished her stepdaughter to master. 'I will show you to your room.'

Catherine followed her up the staircase, not quite knowing what to say. The slim, ramrod-straight back was as hostile-looking as Doña Lucía's eyes had been only a moment before, and she led the way along the gallery without another word. Here and there large items of Spanish furniture placed against the whitewashed walls cast even darker shadows on their way, and the heavy oak doors

leading to the upstairs rooms were all carefully closed
against intrusion, giving what should have been a happy
family residence the air of a prison. She remembered what
Teresa had said about Soria in Madrid, thinking that it
was all understandable now that she had come here.

Lucía paused at an archway leading to a suite of rooms
beyond the gallery.

'You will be here, with Teresa,' she announced. 'Out of
harm's way.'

It was an odd remark to make, but Catherine was not in
a position to question it at the moment. Lucía flung open
one of the doors beyond the arch, standing aside so that
she might go in, and Catherine had the impression of a
sparsely-furnished room which yet was adequate for her
requirements, with bright chintz curtains at the windows
and the inevitable four-poster bed against one wall.

'It's lovely,' she said. 'Thank you, Doña Lucía. I shall be
very comfortable, I'm sure.'

She looked up into the unresponsive face, but all she
could see was the ruby lying like a spot of blood at Lucía's
throat and the eyes above it burning with hatred as Teresa
came slowly towards them along the gallery.

'*Buenas noches, madrastra!*' said Teresa. 'I hope you are
now well.'

'Well enough, in the way you mean.' Lucía had frowned
at the word 'stepmother' but let it pass. 'Of course, I am
still mourning your father's death, as no one else here
seems to do.'

A deep red colour stained Teresa's cheeks.

'We all grieve for him, *madrastra*, but we do not all wear
our hearts on our sleeves,' she said. 'I will never forget him,
although it is three years now since he was killed.'

'Three years is nothing!' Doña Lucía turned to leave
them. 'You had a pleasant stay in Madrid?' she asked with
pointed courtesy.

'Very pleasant. You know I always like to go there,'
Teresa said.

Her stepmother laughed unpleasantly.

'I know that you like to put as many miles as possible between us,' she conceded, 'but you cannot do as you like until you are eighteen and your own mistress.'

The flush deepened in Teresa's cheeks.

'You remind me of the fact so often, *madrastra*, that I am hardly likely to forget,' she countered, 'yet you will be glad to be rid of me when the time comes.'

A guarded look came into Lucía's eyes.

'You know that Jaime wishes you to remain here,' she said in an altered voice. 'He is responsible for you until you come of age. He made a promise to your father before he died.'

Without waiting for her stepdaughter's answer she swept away along the gallery to her own room, closing the door firmly behind her.

There was a small, awkward pause as Teresa and Catherine looked at each other.

'She does not like you,' Teresa said, at last, 'because you are young and beautiful and because you may one day attract Jaime.' A spark of glee dawned in her dark eyes. 'That would be something worth waiting for,' she declared. 'Doña Lucía in second place! Why are you blushing, Cathy?' she demanded. 'Surely you know that you are beautiful with your fiery hair and skin like a ripe peach and a figure almost as slim as Lucía's? She is not in the least beautiful except, perhaps, for her hair which she attends to so lovingly. Do you not think that her face is too long and her eyes too near together? Besides, she has the Velázquez nose, which is too high and too sharp to be attractive in a woman.'

Teresa's description of her stepmother had been apt but decidedly cruel, and Catherine would not encourage her.

'I thought her distinguished,' she answered carefully. 'Does she always wear that magnificent ruby at her throat?'

It was the wrong question to ask. Teresa's eyes filled with angry tears.

'It belonged to my mother,' she gulped, 'but my father gave it to Lucía on their wedding day. It is the Pablo ruby and it should have been mine. It has been handed down in my mother's family for many years.'

Wondering if this might be the main cause of dissension between Teresa and her stepmother, Catherine began to unpack her suitcases, hanging up her dresses once more in a capacious wardrobe and folding her underwear neatly in the dressing-chest drawer. For how long this time? Doña Lucía's dislike of her seemed to hang above her head like the Sword of Damocles, yet it would be Don Jaime who would finally ask her to go.

She crossed to the windows to look out, opening one of them to step out on to the creeper-covered balcony which overhung part of the *patio*, and suddenly the scent of stephanotis was all around her. It hung in the still air like incense, cloying, overwhelming, dangerously sweet, holding her there in the darkness until she was aware of a movement on the terrace beyond the thin silver thread of the fountain. A man and a woman were standing out there, half in shadow, half revealed, and the woman was too tall to be anyone but Lucía.

Catherine stepped back involuntarily. Lucía and Don Jaime? She could not see the man plainly enough, but the two were undoubtedly deep in conversation until Lucía finally made a gesture of dismissal and the second figure dissolved into the shadows cast by the motionless palms. Lucía came towards the house along the colonnaded stretch of the *patio*, glimpsed here and there before she finally disappeared inside, but once she had gone from the terrace her companion of a few minutes ago returned. It was not Don Jaime. The man was shorter and more sturdily built and he wore a *poncho* over his clothes, as if he had just come in after a long journey. The horse he had been riding followed him out of the shadows, led on a long rein.

Catherine drew a sharp breath of relief, although why she should have thought that it was Don Jaime down there on the terrace when he could have spoken with Lucía openly in the house she could not imagine.

CHAPTER THREE

THE meal they shared at ten o'clock that evening was traditionally Spanish. It was served in the long, whitewashed dining-room whose windows opened on to the colonnaded end of the *patio* overlooking the fountain, and the superb black oak refectory table and high-backed chairs with their intricate carving were a joy to Catherine as she took her place beside Ramón, who seemed to be in excellent spirits now that his young niece was safely home.

Teresa sat facing them with her back to the windows, and Don Jaime settled Lucía in the armchair at the foot of the table. He himself sat down at the head, very much the master in his own house, saying grace with an authority which stopped Teresa in her tracks as she began to speak.

'I had forgotten,' she apologised when he had finished. 'In Madrid people do not always say grace.'

' "There is only one place better than Madrid and that is Heaven?" ' Ramón quoted teasingly, but she chose to ignore him.

The servants entered with their first course, led by Eugénie carrying a huge tureen of soup while Alfredo followed with a tray of ice-cooled melon and the delicious *jamón serrano* which Catherine had already sampled in Madrid. The dark red mountain ham, cured in the sun, would be at its best here, she thought, as Eugénie put the tureen down on the table in front of Lucía and handed her the silver serving ladle.

'What has happened to Manuel?' Ramón asked as they ate. 'I did not see him come in.'

Lucía stiffened.

'Surely it is not of great importance what becomes of Manuel,' she suggested icily. 'He comes and goes as he wishes, attending to the horses, as he is meant to do.'

Ramón opened his mouth to reply, but decided against the impulse.

'I hope he has been looking after Seda for me while I've been away,' Teresa remarked.

'Every day,' Lucía observed drily, 'but do we have to talk about Manuel all the time? He does his job at Soria and that is all we have to be concerned about.'

'So long as he does it well,' Don Jaime agreed, serving Catherine with a portion of the delicious mountain ham sliced so thinly as to be almost transparent. 'I will see him in the morning about the horses.'

'Cathy ought to have a horse to ride,' Teresa suggested. 'It is the only way to get around the estate when all the cars are in use.'

'Can you ride?' Don Jaime looked round at Catherine with a hint of doubt in his eyes.

'Not very well,' she was forced to confess. 'I didn't live that sort of life in England. My home was in London.'

'Everyone rides here,' Ramón interjected. 'I will teach you, Cathy.'

Don Jaime frowned.

'I think we will rely on Manuel,' he said drily. 'You have other work to do.'

A quick flash of resentment sparked in his brother's eyes.

'You must know that all work and no play makes Jack a dull boy,' he said, 'but I will concede that Manuel does the teaching while I supply Cathy with the experience—in my free time.'

Their gaze met over the silver candelabrum which adorned the table, the small flames of the candles reflected in their eyes as they confronted one another on yet another issue, before Ramón laughed.

'Have no fear, Jaime,' he said. 'I am not rash enough to imagine that I will make a conquest immediately. Cathy will be hard to win!'

Catherine felt distinctly uncomfortable. The others were looking at her, Teresa with amusement, Lucía with frank distaste, and Don Jaime with something like anger in his

eyes. No one answered Ramón's foolish boast, but the un-
guarded remark suggested that he might be the gay
Lothario of the family, the youngest son encouraged to be
macho by indulgent parents because they had little more
to offer him. Eduardo had been their heir, and Don Jaime
after him, but a third son would have to rely solely on
his wits and whatever charm he might possess.

The meal ended with large bowls of fresh fruit being
passed round, peaches, dates and sweet Almería grapes, all
grown on the estate, and Don Jaime refilled their glasses
with the smooth white wine which he had poured for the
main course. A good sharp cheese followed with the excellent coffee which Doña Lucía poured at the table.

It was midnight before they finally rose to go to bed
and Lucía, as befitted the hostess, lingered in the *sala*
while the others moved towards the staircase.

'Jaime,' she said briskly, 'may I speak with you for a
moment?'

Don Jaime turned back towards the fireplace where they
had all been sitting discussing Madrid.

'Now, out will come all the complaints!' Teresa murmured. 'Jaime will have to listen to every little detail of
domestic upheaval until she gets it all out of her system.
Also——'

She paused and Catherine turned to look at her.

'There's you and me,' Teresa added. 'Neither of us
pleases my stepmother. I never have, and you have just
come as a great shock to her. She expected you to be
middle-aged and plain.'

'Everyone did,' Catherine sighed. 'Even Don Jaime. When
he first met me at the airport I thought he was about to
send me straight back to London on the next flight.'

'The Marquesa would not have it, and I am glad,'
Teresa declared, linking her arm in Catherine's. 'It is good
to have someone young to talk to.'

'Your stepmother isn't exactly old,' Catherine pointed
out.

'She's twenty-nine,' Teresa returned briskly. 'One year

older than Jaime. She married my father when she was twenty-five because no one else had spoken for her.'

'Must a girl still be "spoken for" in Spain?' Catherine asked doubtfully.

'Not always. We are more emancipated now and can choose for ourselves, but Lucía came from a very strict family and she had lived all her life in the country. She was very old-fashioned, but always she was jealous. It is a very dangerous thing to be, don't you think?' She paused by the bedroom door.

'Carried to excess,' Catherine admitted.

Ramón, who had followed them up the staircase, came to say a final goodnight.

'Still gossiping!' he observed. 'You will not be able to rise early in the morning if you stay up half the night talking.' He held Catherine's friendly smile. 'Let me take you riding tomorrow, *señorita*,' he begged. 'I will show you the *hacienda* at its best.'

'You will not!' Teresa exclaimed. 'I am going to do that and, besides, Cathy has no skill in riding. She must go quietly at first, and you are a demon on horseback, Ramón!'

'Would you prefer that I ride a little donkey?' he mocked. 'You do not like it because I can handle a horse better than you!' He was openly teasing now. 'We will find Cathy a gentle mount and all will be well.'

'You must remember that I have come here to work,' Catherine protested.

'Oh, work!' Teresa frowned. 'I have too much of that already.'

'You will return to the convent in the autumn,' her uncle pointed out, 'and then you will have to work.'

The pregnant silence with which Teresa met his challenge suggested that she would resist a return to her schooldays with all her might.

'We shall see,' she said stubbornly. 'I shall be seventeen before the autumn and quite grown up.'

'I must wait around to see that day!' Ramón grinned. '*Buenas noches*, Cathy—until tomorrow!'

As he left them to walk round the gallery to the other side of the house Don Jaime and his sister-in-law came to the foot of the stairs, and suddenly Catherine felt her gaze drawn downwards to where they stood. Don Jaime was frowning as he watched his brother's progress along the gallery and then he turned and went out through the *patio* doors into the star-filled night.

In the morning Catherine was last down to breakfast because it had been almost two o'clock before she had finally fallen asleep.

'I've disgraced myself,' she said, glancing at the used plates on the circular table in the morning-room. 'Everyone seems to have gone to work.'

She was thinking of Don Jaime more than anyone else, wondering what he might have had to say about her late appearance.

'Oh, Jaime and Ramón leave at the crack of dawn,' Teresa said, helping herself to a ripe peach, 'and Lucía is already about her household tasks. Didn't you hear the noise from the kitchens as you came down? There is always a battle scene first thing in the morning, since nothing is ever quite right for Lucía.'

Her stepmother put in her appearance at the open doorway.

'Ah, you are there, Miss Royce,' she observed, leaving an unspoken 'at last' quivering in the air between them. 'Don Jaime thinks that Teresa and you should have the use of a study for your work.' She had stressed the final word. 'I have arranged that this should be so and Teresa will show you the small *salón* which I can put at your disposal while you remain here.'

In the full, clear morning light she looked older than her twenty-nine years, but there was no doubt about the beauty of the long, blue-black hair which she wore coiled regally about her head. It was her crowning glory, and this morning she had dressed it even higher with a magnificent tortoiseshell comb thrust into the plait at the back, adding extra height to her slim, taut figure as she stood waiting for Catherine's reply. The sun was shining and birds were flitting among the garden trees while the scent of a thousand flowers filled the air. It was a day to be out in the open, but Lucía had stressed the fact that the English girl had come to Soria to work.

'Thank you,' said Catherine. 'I'll arrange my books there as soon as they arrive.'

Lucía hesitated in the doorway.

'Surely Teresa has sufficient books of her own,' she suggested. 'I seem to remember that her father was always buying her books of one kind or another when he visited Madrid, but Don Jaime has spoken to me about the books you expect to arrive and I will see that they are delivered to you immediately.'

It was as if they were living in separate establishments, Catherine thought, noticing that Lucía was still wearing the ruby which had been her sole adornment the evening before. In the bright sunshine it gleamed against the dark background of her dress like a malevolent eye, absorbing the light to fling it back in shafts of living flame which were almost dazzling to the eye. Not a jewel to be worn first thing in the morning, Catherine would have thought, reminding herself in the next breath that Lucía's ruby was no affair of hers.

'We can work in the open on the shaded end of the *patio* outside the *salón* windows,' Teresa suggested when they were left alone. 'Lucía must have her little say, but it amounts to nothing. Jaime will not object to us studying in the fresh air or even riding while we talk. We will not even have to consult him.'

They spent the entire morning arranging the little *salón* for their own use. It was an intimate little room at the far end of the *patio*, its windows shaded by the overgrown creeper which cascaded from the tiled roof of the colonnaded walkway leading on to the terraces, and the view of the valley it commanded was truly magnificent. Time slipped away pleasantly until Teresa pointed out that it was one o'clock.

'Let's eat here,' she suggested. 'It will be fun doing as we please.'

Already some of the sullen expression had left her face; she smiled more often and had been far more communicative as they had planned a suitable schedule for their daily work, even offering a suggestion or two of her own to augment Catherine's quite lengthy list of plays and books to be read, although she still insisted that they should often ride together.

'You must try on a pair of my jodhpurs,' she suggested, standing up to measure their respective heights. 'They're going to be wide round the middle,' she sighed regretfully, 'but you can always belt them in.'

Catherine wondered what her uncle might have to say about the riding lessons, but certainly they needn't involve Ramón or keep him from his work on the estate.

Teresa went to order their lunch, which was brought to them on a tray by Sisa and laid out on the low stone wall of the *patio* among the flowers. It was a lovely setting, light and shade alternating along the entire length of the colonnades, with the dazzling brilliance of the sun beyond and, far in the distance, the ever-present peak of El Teide rising against the cloudless blue of the sky.

'*Pulpitos!*' Teresa exclaimed, raising the lid of a covered dish to reveal a quantity of fried squid. 'Jaime likes them served "in their ink", but Lucía orders them as a special dish for him. He does not often come back at midday unless he has to telephone to Santa Cruz or the *puerto*. It will be *cocido* tonight because he is also fond of that.'

Lucía obviously did her best to please her brother-in-law, giving her orders accordingly, and they heard her haranguing the servants as they made their way across the hall half an hour later.

'There she goes!' Teresa declared. 'The exacting mistress of Soria who never lets one single detail escape her eagle eye!' Then, on a sudden change of mood, she added lightly: 'Come to my room as soon as you have taken your *siesta* and you can try on my riding trousers. Then I shall tell

Manuel to bring round the horses.'

Unused to sleeping during the day, Catherine spent the next hour rearranging her room to draw the small writing-desk nearer to the window and place a chair up there, too. Sunshine was too precious a thing in her English eyes to waste, however, and she was soon out on her balcony looking out across the garden to the terraces below and beyond them to the distant sea. On either side of the vines another sea of waving banana fronds stirred languidly before a little errant breeze which stole down from El Teide, but otherwise the world was very still. In the quiet *siesta* hour the *patio* lay peacefully in the shadow of its overhanging eaves with only a fat green lizard darting occasionally among the stones. She thought of Lucía and the man in the enveloping *poncho* who had met and talked secretly down there the evening before. It could have been anyone—a servant, a male acquaintance reluctant to gatecrash the family reunion on Don Jaime's return—yet surely there should have been no great need for secrecy.

Another man made his appearance at the end of the terrace wall and she drew back with a gasp as he rode towards her. It was Don Jaime seated on a magnificent Arab horse, the Conquistador himself.

She had never seen him on horseback before, but this was surely his true element. Tall and straight, he sat easily in the saddle, one strong hand controlling the rein, the other negligently by his side, his proud head averted as his eagle gaze scanned the vast extent of his possessions. He had ridden long in the heat, it seemed, because the soft leather boots he wore were covered in the fine red dust of the valley, but he did not appear to be in need of the *siesta* which everyone else enjoyed.

She listened to the sound of the approaching horse as it negotiated the brick-paved road to the stables, but suddenly it was arrested. The Arab's head was turned in her direction and Don Jaime de Berceo Madroza was looking up at her in full sunlight. Her heart seemed to miss a beat

as he took off his wide-brimmed Córdoban hat and swept
her a mocking bow.

'I thought you would have been asleep,' he said.

'I never sleep in the middle of the day.'

'That is very unwise of you. What have you been doing
all morning?'

'Arranging the "schoolroom". Teresa and I will begin
work there tomorrow in earnest.'

'Have you everything you need? If not, you must ask
Lucía or Manuel.'

'Teresa thought we might ride a short distance later in
the afternoon,' she said tentatively.

'Why not? You can't be expected to work all day.
Teresa, for one, would not agree! Besides, when you are
riding together you can be talking together, but I thought
you told me that you did not ride very well.'

'Teresa thinks I should learn.'

'So you shall. I will speak to Manuel about a suitable
mount for you, one that will not run away with you the
very first time.'

He seemed to be faintly amused by the thought of someone who could not ride, but he had been brought up with
all the privileges, she told herself angrily.

'Perhaps I would be safer on a mule,' she suggested.

'Mules can prove much more difficult to ride if they have
the proverbial stubborn streak in them,' he assured her,
dismounting from his magnificent white horse. 'You may
have to use one occasionally—if you go to Las Cañadas,
for instance, to climb El Teide in the traditional manner—
but for the present I would stick to one of the ponies, if I
were you. I will speak to Manuel.'

He paused, still looking up at her, his dark head un-
covered, his deeply-tanned face thoughtful for a moment,
and suddenly the scent of stephanotis was all about them,
too strong for Catherine to bear. She drew back into the
shelter of her room as he led the horse away.

Five minutes later, Teresa was calling to her from her
own bedroom.

'Come and try these on,' she commanded when Catherine made her appearance at the adjacent door. 'I haven't
worn them for a long time, so they should almost fit.'

She held out a pair of yellow jodhpurs made from very
fine cavalry twill and patched on the inside of the leg with
a pale skin as delicate as chamois, which possibly came
from the local goats roaming in abundance among the
hills.

'Are you sure?' Catherine asked, laughing as her eye
caught the inscription blazoned in lipstick across Teresa's
dressing-table mirror.

'CAKES ARE DANGEROUS', the younger girl had printed
in letters a foot high.

'I have to be constantly reminded,' she confessed. 'Do
you think I will ever slim?'

'If you try hard enough you will soon be asking for those
back.' Catherine had slipped into the perfectly-fitting
jodhpurs to survey herself in what was left of the mirror.
'Thank you for being so kind, Teresa.'

They went downstairs and out to the courtyard to find
Lucía there with Don Jaime.

'But I shall need Manuel this afternoon,' Lucía was saying. 'I wish him to carry the flowerpots to the *patio* for
me.'

'You have Alfredo to fall back on,' her brother-in-law
pointed out. 'I am sure he is quite as efficient as Manuel
when it comes to carrying flowerpots.'

His suave rejoinder seemed to madden Lucía.

'Manuel is my personal servant!' she exclaimed furiously.
'I will not have him used for—anyone else.'

It was evident that she meant Catherine, and suddenly
the atmosphere became electric as Manuel led two well-
groomed ponies into the courtyard. Catherine turned to
look at him. He was small and dark and intense, with a
magnetism about him which she found hard to describe
as she gazed back into his coal-black eyes. He was the man
in the *poncho* whom Lucía had met so clandestinely in the
shadowed colonnades of the *patio* the evening before.

There could be no doubt about it. The small figure in
the gaily-coloured blanket was unmistakable, although now
Manuel stood back obediently, waiting for his mistress's
command.

'You will go with the *señoritas* this afternoon, Manuel,'
Don Jaime told him, 'and you will lead Vivo most of the
way.' He turned back to Catherine. 'Vivo is one of our
quieter ponies,' he assured her. 'His speed belies his name.'

'I hope so,' Catherine smiled. 'I've only been on a horse
once before and I don't think he really took to me.'

He laughed.

'Vivo will be your friend if you handle him properly.' He
cast an expert eye over her trim figure, obviously approv-
ing the borrowed jodhpurs.

'Teresa lent them to me,' she explained.

Manuel was standing beside the pony, waiting to help
her into the saddle, but his master stepped forward to hold
the stirrup for her. Suddenly the little animal seemed
enormous, but she would not let Don Jaime see how nervous she was. Besides, Lucía was looking on with faint scorn
in her eyes. I'll do it as gracefully as I can, Catherine
thought, glancing sideways at the ancient mounting-block
which nobody seemed to use.

'Up you go!' said Don Jaime, supporting her until she
was safely in the saddle.

She sat there holding her breath for a moment after
that initial effort, but whether it was at the touch of his
hand or from nervousness of a new experience was difficult
to say. Teresa leapt on to the back of the other pony, urg-
ing him across the cobbles with a disdainful look in
Manuel's direction which dared him to suggest a leading-
rein, but Catherine was glad of the young Spaniard's quiet
assurance as he led Vivo slowly away.

Looking back as they rounded the gable end of the
house, she saw Lucía turn angrily along the *patio*, but Don
Jaime stood watching their progress until they were finally
out of sight.

Manuel, mounted on his own shaggy pony, kept the

leading-rein firmly in his hand, a fact for which she was grateful as Teresa took off at some speed in the direction of the door through which they had entered the afternoon before. Waiting for Manuel to open it, she looked down at him with some scorn.

'You have no need to be silent, Manuel,' she said. 'I know you can speak English quite well and will listen to everything we say.'

A quick flush stained the young Spaniard's brow.

'I do not come to spy, señorita,' he returned with some spirit, 'even if that is what you think of me. Always I perform my duties as I am supposed to do, and I am not your servant.'

The quiet dignity of the man spoke volumes. He had been more or less accused of being Lucía's informer, but he would have none of it. There was injured pride in the dark eyes as they looked back into Teresa's and a certain amount of boldness which Catherine found strangely disquieting. He was young, he was handsome, and he had a fiery temper which only seemed to be subdued in Lucía's presence. He was her personal servant, but there was something more than that between them. In public Lucía treated him with a haughtiness relevant to their respective stations, but the evening before they had stood close in the garden beside the fountain, half hidden in the shadows of the colonnade, half revealed as the moon fled across the sky.

For an hour they rode along the narrow dirt road which skirted the *hacienda* wall, passing tiny *adobe* houses smothered in vines and great packing-sheds where the estate workers were busy in the cool dimness of the cavern-like interiors packing a consignment of bananas for the journey to Santa Cruz in the morning. Several lorries with the Madroza name on their sides waited, ready to be loaded, the drivers sleeping soundly beneath them, out of the sun. Teresa flicked her riding-whip.

'If Jaime came along they would think of something better to do,' she declared. 'Ramón will not tell them to work harder. He is too eager to be one of them and drive on a lorry to Santa Cruz.'

They halted where the road began to climb out of the valley, sitting in the shade of a young dragon tree to survey the vast panorama of terraced vines and bananas spread out beneath them. It was a whole kingdom, Catherine thought, bounded on the north by that high brick wall which must have taken years of patient labour to build and by the distant sea in the south. Until now, she had had no idea how vast the Madroza possessions were, and even her untrained eye could see that the irrigation dykes had been newly maintained so that a regular flow of water would enrich the land. If all this had been Don Jaime's doing he had every reason to feel satisfied.

'My father did much to enhance the estate,' Teresa said proudly, 'but Jaime has also worked very hard. At one time Soria was badly neglected; there was no money to put back into the land.' Her voice hardened. 'The necessary money came with Lucía. Her father was a rich merchant and she was his only daughter.'

So Soria owed much to Lucía in a material way and Don Jaime, if not Teresa, would be grateful.

As they reached the high road and were approaching the first of the packing-stations a cloud of red dust ahead of them announced the presence of a horse and rider travelling at speed.

'It's Ramón,' said Teresa, 'making up time.'

The rider emerged from the red cloud into the sunlight of the dirt road as they reached the sheds, drawing up abruptly when he saw them.

'Where have you been?' Teresa demanded. 'To the Gran Hotel los Dogos, I suppose.'

'You suppose wrongly, but I did go to the *puerto*,' Ramón admitted, obviously looking for someone else. 'Has Jaime been around?' he asked casually.

'Luckily for you, he hasn't,' Teresa returned. 'It's a working day, or hadn't you noticed?'

Ramón gave her a disparaging look.

'I was up at the crack of dawn,' he informed her, 'long before you were even awake.' Brushing some of the dust from his clothes, he dismounted, coming to stand beside Catherine. 'Did my brother approve the pony?' he enquired, looking up at her with one dark eye closed against the sunlight. 'Vivo is very tame.'

Catherine glanced sideways at the powerful horse he had been riding. It was the colour of sand and would be hardly noticeable in the high reaches of the mountains, a spirited animal now pawing the ground restlessly as he waited.

'I'm a very indifferent horsewoman, so Vivo suits me very well,' she said. 'You must have ridden most of your life.'

'My father used to say I was practically born in the saddle,' Ramón acknowledged. 'My mother was a fearless horsewoman, although most women rode behind their husbands in those days. Teresa takes after her,' he added. 'She is her true *nieta*, full of spirit and wilfulness which my brother does his best to curb.'

Teresa got down from her pony to stretch her legs.

'Why is it always a girl who must be subdued?' she demanded. 'You are not exactly placid, Ramón, but you have a very good way of hiding it which is perhaps what I need.'

'I wouldn't try anything on with Jaime, if I were you,' he warned her with a half-smile. 'He is not easily deceived.' He turned to help Catherine from the saddle. 'You must need a rest,' he suggested.

'If I get down I'm never going to be able to mount again,' Catherine declared. 'As it is, I feel permanently bent in the middle!'

He was standing close beneath her, one hand on the pony's glossy flank, the other on the stirrup, and there was a small flame of anticipation in his eyes as he looked up at her.

'Come with me to the *puerto* this evening,' he begged. 'I will show you what life on this remote little island can really be like.'

'The *puerto* is no longer Tenerife,' Teresa declared with amazing candour. 'You would not be showing her the true island, only a few sophisticated hotels.'

'You're jealous,' Ramón shot back, 'because it is out of bounds as far as you are concerned. But perhaps we can all go,' he added. 'I ran into Alex Bonnington while I was down there this morning and she was greatly impressed by Cathy. She would like us to visit her. Lucía, too, of course,' he added. 'Alex is nothing if not polite.'

Catherine had liked Alex Bonnington on sight, feeling that the advice and friendship of a fellow-countrywoman might not come amiss during her stay at Soria. She had been vaguely troubled by Alex's warning, however, but since she was not going to stay at the *hacienda* for the rest of her life it didn't seem to matter very much.

'Perhaps we could learn to paint,' Teresa suggested. 'At least that would be something different to do. Oh, here comes Jaime,' she added. 'In a bit of a hurry, by the looks of things.'

Ramón did not move. When his brother rode up he was still standing with his hand on Catherine's stirrup, looking up at her, something insolent in his manner now that he was discovered idling away his time in conversation.

Wondering why she should also feel guilty, Catherine looked over the pony's shaggy head into Don Jaime's hostile eyes, and for a moment he held her gaze before he rode into the shade of the packing sheds to dismount.

'There are four lorries at San Bartolomé waiting to start for Santa Cruz,' he said to Ramón. 'None of them have the necessary bills of lading. Can you advise me what has happened to them, or is that too much to ask on a pleasant afternoon when you have other distractions to take up your time?'

'Heavens, I forgot!' Ramón looked truly contrite. 'I meant to see to the bills yesterday, but it slipped my mind.' He vaulted on to his horse. 'It won't take me long to get them. They're back at the house.'

He turned on a tight rein to gallop off by the way he had

come and something about the sharp, contrary movement seemed to disturb Catherine's pony. The docile little animal shivered where he stood and then, without warning, he took to his heels and flew off in the wake of Ramón and his spirited steed.

Taken completely by surprise and sickeningly aware that Manuel had let go of the leading-rein while they had stood talking, she flung her arms around the pony's neck and clung on like grim death, praying that the little animal would stop of his own accord before final disaster overtook them. The narrow road with its fringe of palms and scrub flashed past her as the thunder of heavier hooves came up behind them.

Don Jaime spoke sharply in his own language and the pony slackened its pace and was soon standing still by the roadside. Catherine turned her head sideways to look at her rescuer.

'I'm sorry,' she managed because it always seemed necessary to apologise for her actions. 'I couldn't stop him once he got going.'

'Get down,' Don Jaime ordered.

She saw how hard his mouth was.

'I can't!' She was still clinging to the pony's neck.

'Certainly you can.' He dismounted, but he did not try to help her. 'You will strangle the horse if you don't let go.'

Cautiously she regained an upright position, straightening in the saddle.

'Now take your foot out of the stirrup and swing towards me,' he commanded. 'I will not let you fall.'

What a fool he must think her! Catherine bit her lip and obeyed his instructions, leaning heavily against his shoulder as she struggled to remove her foot from the second stirrup. In an instant his arms were about her, holding her securely before he finally put her on the ground.

'What an exhibition!' She tried to laugh. 'I told you I wasn't very good on a horse.'

She was trembling visibly, aware of his nearness and the

contact of their two bodies as he had held her for that one brief second in time.

'You have had a nasty shock,' he said quite gently.

Was that all? His hands were still on her arms, his face close as he looked down at her with genuine concern in his eyes, but after a moment he put her gently away from him, steadying her on her feet, although he must have been aware that she was still trembling.

She wanted to explain how terrified she had been but couldn't. Her heart was pounding madly, and every nerve in her body seemed to be jarred, yet in that first moment when his arms had closed about her she had felt secure.

The clamour in her heart would not die down, even now that there was no further cause for alarm. Physically she was safe enough and probably there had been no real danger. She tried to meet his eyes complacently, but her errant heartbeats seemed to fill the silence between them with overwhelming sound.

'You must get straight back into the saddle,' he advised in a matter-of-fact tone which steadied her a little. 'It is the only way. If you allow yourself to be afraid now you will never ride successfully.'

She hardly heard what he said, turning her head away, still conscious of the pounding of her own heart. I can't fall in love with him, she thought. I couldn't complicate a situation which is already dangerous enough!

'I'm all right now,' she managed to say. 'It's like—riding a bicycle, isn't it? One spill shouldn't mean defeat.'

'Let me help you,' he said, cupping his hands to assist her into the saddle. 'We must be thankful that nothing more serious has befallen you.'

'Don't blame Ramón too much,' she begged, meeting his eyes with a quiet entreaty in her own. 'It wasn't really his fault.'

'Ramón is always going off at a tangent,' he said. 'I dare say he has no idea what happened.' His dark gaze swept the empty road ahead of them. 'He will be almost home by now.'

'I should have been more attentive,' she blamed herself. 'I never dreamed that Vivo would actually bolt.'

Her words dropped into a little confused silence while he looked up at her.

'All right now?' he asked as Teresa and Manuel appeared round a bend in the road.

'Quite all right, thank you.' She had cleared her voice to answer him with confidence. 'I won't make the same mistake again.'

'Cathy!' Teresa cried when they were within hailing distance, 'Are you all in one piece?' She looked greatly relieved when she saw Catherine still in the saddle. 'You gave us a great fright, I must say, but now it seems that you have not taken any harm, after all.' She began to laugh. 'If you had seen yourself!' she exclaimed. 'All yellow bottom and flying hair! I thought you were going to strangle poor Vivo before you fell off!' She looked from Catherine to her silent uncle. 'Did you fall off?' she enquired tentatively. 'Or did Jaime catch you?'

'He caught up with me,' Catherine allowed, made suddenly uncomfortable by the speculative look in Teresa's eyes. 'I think I was ready to fall,' she added lightly, 'but he saved me the indignity.'

'Will you ride home with us now?' Teresa asked Don Jaime. 'Perhaps you do not trust us to go carefully any more.'

'I have other things to see to,' he assured her, 'but I will be home quite soon. You may tell Ramón that I will be waiting at San Bartolomé.'

He would not return home until the last lorry with its consignment of bananas was well on its way to Santa Cruz, and no doubt Ramón would be kept working later than usual to make up for his unexplained visit to the *puerto*. The two brothers were evidently not seeing eye to eye about Soria, and possibly there was another bone of contention between them. Ramón was something of a philanderer, a charming latter-day Don Juan whose idle lovemaking would incense a man of Jaime de Berceo Madroza's calibre and make him impatient, to say the least. What, then, must he have thought when he had come across the little tableau outside the packing-sheds? Ramón had been standing in the centre of the group holding Catherine's stirrup while he looked up at her with frank admiration in his eyes, and Catherine knew that she had responded with a happy smile. Ramón was so easy to like, but the fact that his work had been neglected would be far more important in his brother's eyes.

When they were almost at the high wooden door in the surrounding wall they met Ramón riding swiftly in the opposite direction.

'I'll be back in under an hour,' he promised, 'and then we will have some music. Jaime cannot possibly work in the dark!'

He flourished the mislaid bills of lading as he rode off in his efforts to make amends for his irresponsible forgetfulness.

'Ramón will never make a farmer,' Teresa commented as they rode in under the creeper-covered arch. 'Jaime should let him go to Santa Cruz or Madrid.'

'He must need him on the estate,' Catherine found herself saying. 'Otherwise, I think he would let him go.'

Teresa drew a deep breath which was half a sigh.

'How little you know of Jaime,' she said. 'If he thinks it will be best for Soria he will keep Ramón here for ever. But perhaps if he marries Lucía, Ramón will be free to go.'

There was an abrupt movement at Catherine's side as Manuel dismounted to lead her pony across the cobbled yard. Half hidden by the wide-brimmed hat he wore, she could not see his face from where she sat in the saddle, but something about his hunched shoulders and the way he moved suggested despair and an inner abandonment to grief.

Lucía was waiting for them on the *patio*. She had changed out of her habitual black dress into a long evening gown of some soft, clinging material, not grey, not blue, but somewhere between the two colours, which was

both mysterious and attractive allied to her jet-black hair
and sombre dark-lashed eyes. Once again her only jewel
was the magnificent ruby which she wore close to her
throat.

Manuel, who was leading the ponies, stopped in his
tracks to look at her, the light of adoration burning in his
eyes, though he thought that none could see.

'What is the matter with you, Manuel?' Lucía asked
imperiously. 'Why do you stare? Are you afraid to be re-
primanded for some indiscretion or other? You are like a
nervous *peón* who has not done his work properly.'

The fact that she had reduced him to the status of a
field labourer sent a wild colour into her servant's cheeks.

'I have only done your will, *señora*,' he said with admir-
able patience. 'I can do no more.'

'Then be off with you!' Lucía commanded, amused by
the havoc she had wrought. 'I will ride tomorrow morning
early,' she added, 'before the sun is strong.'

'*Sí, señora.*'

He led the ponies away across the yard and Catherine
was suddenly overwhelmingly sorry for him. Poor Manuel,
who dared to love the lady he served! Poor Manuel, des-
tined to worship her for ever with no hope of love in return!

'You look dishevelled,' Lucía observed, glancing in her
direction. 'Have you met with an accident?'

'Not quite. Vivo took fright and bolted, but he did not
go very fast or very far,' Catherine explained.

'Jaime rescued her,' Teresa interposed. 'He was off in
pursuit before Manuel or I were in the saddle. I think he
imagined she might be killed.'

Lucía turned away with an angry gesture which indi-
cated that she had no desire to hear the details of their
little adventure or to learn exactly how her brother-in-law
had come to the rescue.

'In future I think you had better ride inside the walls,
Miss Royce,' she suggested coldly. 'The valley roads are
too rough for a—novice.'

'We'd better go and change,' Teresa decided, 'and then we can listen to Ramón's music. He plays quite well, as a matter of fact, and sings like an angel.'

An hour later the sound of a guitar played softly beneath her window took Catherine on to her balcony, although she did not look beyond it to discover who might be serenading her so romantically by the light of the moon. She knew that it was Ramón and she listened half impatiently until the poignant love song came to an end. It finished on a long-drawn-out note, like a sigh, and something of its intensity lingered in the still night air before Ramón broke into the lively music of a gay Catalan *sardana*. All the Spanish dances had their own individuality and charm and soon her foot was tapping out the rhythm of the tune she already knew.

'Come down,' Ramón called to her softly when he had ceased to play. 'It is better if I can see you than just knowing that you are there.'

'Don Juan in person!' Teresa observed, coming into the bedroom behind her.

Catherine swung round, unable to control the swift rush of colour which rose to her cheeks.

'He plays beautifully,' she remarked lamely.

'Too beautifully at times! Ramón could charm a heart of stone with his music, and he uses it shamelessly for his own ends. You must not take him too seriously,' Teresa warned, 'because Ramón is not serious all the time. Guitar music is meant for lovers,' she added, 'but only if they are truly in love.'

'How worldly-wise we are tonight!' Catherine pushed back the hair which had fallen over her eyes. 'I like your evening skirt,' she added. 'Is it traditional?'

Teresa pirouetted obligingly to show off the brightly-coloured flounced skirt she wore.

'Traditionally Andalusian,' she agreed. 'Gipsies wear them when they dance *flamenco* round their camp-fires, and fine ladies put them on to ride in open carriages full of flowers at *fiestas* and *ferias*. We have them here, too, you know, though not as many as in Spain.' She skipped towards the door. 'If you are ready we will go down and join Ramón on the *patio*.'

She never referred to Ramón as her uncle, probably because they were too near an age or because she had less respect for him than she had for Don Jaime. He was still playing his guitar when they walked across the polished floor of the hall to the long open windows leading to the *patio*, and he rose to bow mockingly as they approached.

'At last!' he said. 'I have waited almost too long and nearly in despair! What shall I play for you, *señoritas*? A *fandango* or a gay *sardana*, or just another love song? There are so many of them to choose from, you know.'

'Play for me to dance,' Teresa commanded. 'Get me into the mood!'

Ramón hesitated.

'Go on! I am waiting.' She stamped an impatient foot.

Ramón drew his fingers across the strings of his guitar in a preliminary chord.

'What will you dance?'

'The *canto jondo*,' she decided after a moment's consideration.

He raised his eyebrows, but he did not hesitate, sitting down with his back against one of the pillars of the covered way to support the guitar on his knees, and soon the harshly-intense music with its sultry undertones was filling the *patio* and throbbing out into the night.

Teresa backed slowly into the hall, circling it twice with her hands low on her hips, but she did not use them for the first few moments of the dance. All the emotion of the music was reflected on her face as the rhythmic stamping of her heels and the slow movements of her fingers and wrists began, giving vivid life to her performance, and suddenly it seemed as if the quiet *hacienda* had been transformed into a gipsy encampment or some obscure *tasca* where only the pulse of a Romany heartbeat could be heard.

The music quickened as Ramón bent over his guitar and

Teresa's flying feet circled the polished floor. She was using her hands now to emphasis the swift progression of the dance, holding them high above her head and then low, bringing them slowly towards her and thrusting them away as her impatient heels took up the rhythm once more. It seemed as if she had completely forgotten time and place and even her audience in her total absorption with her art, and Catherine could only gaze at her enthralled until she realised that they were no longer alone.

Lucía was watching from the shadows with a calculating look in her eyes.

It was several minutes before Don Jaime came to stand by Catherine's side.

'Teresa feels that she could dance for a living,' he observed, 'but she must first finish her education. When she is older she will be allowed to make her choice.'

'And by then you hope that she will have changed her mind,' Catherine suggested. 'But this may be something she really wants to do, and you could be standing in her way by being so—adamant.'

'You think me lacking in understanding?'

'In a way, yes,' she was forced to admit. 'I think you are judging Teresa by your own standards—a man's standards —and they are not the same.'

'That I do understand,' he said. 'Do you also think I treat my brother too harshly, *señorita*?'

She looked up at him, dismayed.

'I have no right to criticise you,' she admitted, 'but Ramón, too, might be less difficult to handle if you were willing to accept his point of view.'

'For someone who has known us for so short a time, you have come to a great many conclusions,' he said.

Catherine bit her lip.

'You are quite right,' she acknowledged. 'I was being presumptuous.'

He laughed outright.

'I think you might be good for Soria,' he observed. 'Certainly you seem to be good for Teresa. She has taken an interest in her schoolwork again.'

He had dismissed his niece's dancing skill with a shrug as the wild music came to an end and Ramón began to play a love song. The softly-persuasive music wrapped them round, drifting out into the night in a thin tremor of sound until Lucía switched on the wall sconces in the room behind them to flood the *patio* with artificial light.

'If you are ready,' she announced harshly, 'we will take our meal.'

They filed into the panelled dining-room, taking the places at the long table which they had occupied the evening before, Don Jaime at the head and Lucía at the foot, with Catherine and Ramón facing Teresa on either side.

'Where did you really go this afternoon?' Teresa asked, looking across the table at her uncle, who put down his soup-spoon to answer her.

'To the *puerto*, as I have already explained,' he said. 'I went to look for a job.'

The atmosphere became electric.

'And did you get one?' Teresa asked.

'Unfortunately, no. It was already spoken for.'

'If you are so anxious to find a job away from Soria,' Don Jaime suggested, 'we must discuss it.'

Ramón glanced round at him.

'Next time,' he said, hiding his surprise as best he could.

When they rose to take their coffee out on the *patio* he sat down on the low wall, reaching for his guitar again, but the music he played was no longer the music of love. It was quick and bright, a medley of tunes plucked from the strings at random, reflecting the mood which had over-taken him so swiftly. Teresa sat at his feet to listen. They shared the same disposition, Catherine thought; they were like quicksilver, one minute sad, the next delightfully blithe, and nothing Don Jaime or even Lucía could do would ever alter the fact.

CHAPTER FOUR

For the next few days Teresa seemed content to ride within the *hacienda* walls, as Lucía had decreed, and certainly there was plenty of room for exercise. The house itself had been built high on the south-facing side of the valley with the vine terraces stepping down from it in regular rows, and farther down, where the bananas grew in rich profusion, there were narrow roads separating the different years' growth which were ideal for their purpose. Manuel accompanied them for another day, bringing round their ponies when he had unsaddled Lucía's horse, but he had little to say for himself and on the third day Catherine felt that she was capable of riding alone.

'All the same,' Lucía said authoritatively, 'Manuel will go with you. It is an order which I wish to be obeyed.'

So Manuel rode beside them, greatly to Teresa's annoyance, although this time she refrained from making a scene.

Both Jaime and Ramón were too busy to ride for pleasure, but occasionally they came across them on the narrow estate roads or took coffee with them in one of the packing-sheds where the activity had risen to a crescendo of effort as the heat increased.

'It will be almost too hot in the *puerto* now,' Teresa observed on one of these occasions. 'Nearly everyone we know has a house in the mountains to escape the heat, but perhaps we can go to San Juan de la Rambla or Realejo Bajo for the *fiesta*.'

'I'd love that,' Catherine said impulsively. 'Will it be a—family occasion?'

'Oh, dear me, no! Jaime will be far too busy and my stepmother scorns *fiestas*,' Teresa declared. 'We will have to go with Ramón and, perhaps, Manuel, since he appears to be our watchdog.'

She scowled at the inoffensive young man for no very clear reason, but Manuel was either unconscious of her disapproval or determined to ignore it.

They rode on through a grove of olive trees where the road became a mere track covered with stones, and once or twice Catherine was glad of Manuel's assuring hand on the rein when the pony stumbled on the rough surface, shaking his head vigorously to register his protest. Even so, she was riding with more confidence now, conquering the instinctive fear which she had felt when she had first climbed into the saddle. It was really the most natural way of getting around, one that had been used for centuries in this perfect island setting where day followed day in increasing peace.

It was only on very rare occasions that Don Jaime used the family car, and then Lucía drove him to La Laguna to catch a plane for Gran Canaria or one of the other islands where he did business. He was occupied at the moment on the estate itself, however, directing the clearing of the lower plantations, and they saw him in the distance riding his distinctive white Arab horse as they left the shade of the olives to climb back on to the main estate road.

Catherine knew that he would not join them from such a distance when he was so busy, even if he had seen them riding between the rows of olives, and suddenly she felt disappointed.

When they finally reached the house they saw that Lucía was entertaining a visitor. A small white car with an open top was standing at the end of the terrace and Alexandra Bonnington rose to meet them as they approached.

'We saw you riding up through the olives,' she greeted them. 'How nice to meet you again, Miss Royce. But let me call you Cathy,' she suggested with her disarming smile. 'It's so much easier!'

'Of course,' Catherine agreed. 'How is the hand, by the way?'

Alex held out her wrist for inspection.

'Hardly a mark,' she declared—untruthfully, because her skin was still deeply scarred. 'I bleed well but I also heal well! Tell me what you've been doing since we met.'

'Riding mostly, and falling off now and then!' Catherine laughed as Lucía signalled to Manuel to lead away their mounts. 'All the same, I really must persevere because it's a most delightful way of getting about. But I see you prefer to drive.'

'I have no option,' Alex declared, moving her position on the cane settee to let her sit down. 'I wouldn't know what to do with a horse if I owned one, though I used to ride quite well.'

'You can have one of Jaime's horses any time you like,' Teresa assured her, causing her stepmother to frown.

'I may take up the offer one of these days,' Alex decided without a great deal of enthusiasm. 'I really came to ask you to the *fiesta*,' she added. 'You could spend the day with me at Orotava and go down to the coast in the evening when it's not so warm.'

'Cathy would love that,' Teresa said quickly. 'If we were coming to you it would be quite all right.' She glanced sideways at her stepmother without actually asking her permission and Lucía rang for their tea with an angry spark in her eyes.

'You will observe, Alex, that I am rarely consulted in these matters,' she said, 'but I will pass on your invitation to Jaime.' She turned to Catherine for the first time. 'By the way, Miss Royce,' she said, 'your parcel of books has arrived from England. They were sent on from Madrid, although I cannot understand why you should need so many for so short a stay.'

Catherine looked taken aback.

'I thought they might be of some help to Teresa,' she explained. 'They're books I've treasured for a long time.'

'All the more reason why they might have been safer in your own country,' Lucía observed. 'But no matter, they are here and you may wish to unpack them at once to make sure that none of them have been damaged.'

Catherine rose to her feet, the bright colour of embarrassment staining her cheeks. She had been dismissed in the most summary manner, like any other servant. Lucía had used the tone of voice which she reserved for Manuel and Eugénie with the undisguised intention to hurt.

'If you'll excuse me,' she said to Alex, 'I really ought to change, anyway.'

Teresa followed her through the hall.

'I told you what Lucía was like,' she said. 'She really is a viper! She tried to humble you in front of Alex, but it won't make a bit of difference. If Jaime had been there he would have put her in her place.'

'But her "place" is the *hacienda*,' Catherine said in a choked undertone, 'and I have been hired to teach you English.'

'It's not the same,' Teresa declared. 'You are not a servant. I will speak to Jaime about this.'

'Teresa—no!' Catherine protested. 'Please don't create trouble on my behalf.' She drew a deep breath. 'After all, Lucía was quite right. I won't be here for ever.'

Teresa hesitated.

'I want you to be here for a very long time,' she said. 'You are already my friend.'

'Oh, Teresa——!'

Catherine could find nothing more to say because there were sudden tears in her eyes.

Teresa's lips firmed in a determined line.

'When we have washed and changed we will go down to the *patio* together,' she said. 'If we don't, Alex is going to think it strange. I will help you to unpack your books in the morning.'

It seemed the most sensible thing to do, but Catherine found herself lingering over her dressing until Teresa came knocking on her door.

'Hurry!' she admonished when she saw Catherine still in her petticoat. 'Or we will miss Alex altogether.'

There were other voices in the *patio* when they finally

reached it; male voices. Don Jaime and Ramón had come in early from the plantations and had stopped to greet their unexpected visitor while Lucía had ordered fresh coffee to be made. She appeared to be in her element now, the gracious hostess of Soria entertaining on her brother-in-law's behalf, and Catherine could not help noticing the change in her. Lucía was not beautiful in the strictest sense of the word, but her height gave her a presence which she was quick to use and now she was doing her best to be charming.

'I mentioned to Jaime yesterday that it was at least a year since you were here,' she said to Alex. 'Too long a time, really, when we live so near. I know you are a busy person, of course, but you used to take such a delight in coming to the valley to paint.'

Alex looked hastily in Ramón's direction.

'It was a long time ago,' she said. 'I'm on too many committees, that's the trouble. When you're a willing horse they clap a dozen saddles on your back before you realise what's happening, and then you have to wriggle like mad to get them off! I must think of a really splendid excuse to be able to say "No" next time I'm asked!'

'You won't,' Jaime predicted. 'You'll take it on and make a great success of it and all your friends will say "Alex Bonnington can tackle anything and she never makes a mistake!"'

Alex looked down at her slender, artist's hands.

'I've made many mistakes in my life,' she answered quietly. 'Haven't we all?'

Jaime turned abruptly to look down across the terracing.

'That is true,' he said harshly, 'but they are mostly the mistakes of youth and love.'

Alex got up to stand beside him.

'I'm sorry, Jaime,' she apologised under her breath. 'I didn't mean to twist the knife in an old wound.'

Catherine moved to the other side of the *patio*, collecting the used coffee-cups.

'You have no need to do that.' Lucía had come up behind her. 'We have kitchen servants to clear the tables.'

The stinging inference was too obvious to be ignored.

'In my country we are taught to be helpful,' Catherine returned, 'without feeling that we are demeaning ourselves. I came down to say goodbye to Miss Bonnington and I would appreciate a cup of coffee after my long ride.'

Their eyes met, and for a fleeting second there was surprise in Lucía's, followed by what could only be described as venom. Teresa, Catherine remembered, had called her a viper on more than one occasion.

'The coffee is ready,' she announced as Eugénie came in with a huge silver pot in her hand. 'You can set it down here,' she directed, 'and I will pour out.'

Eugénie collected the used cups, smiling as she passed Catherine, a smile of sympathy, perhaps, from one downtrodden employee to another.

Wondering where her sense of humour had gone, Catherine watched as Lucía carried Don Jaime's cup of coffee to the edge of the terrace for him where she set it down on the low stone wall.

'Alex?' she asked. 'Another cup?'

'No, thank you. I must be on my way. Jaime,' Alex added, 'you will bring everyone to the *fiesta*, I hope? You can't pretend to be inundated with work, because all the valley will be on holiday.'

Jaime glanced back to where Catherine was standing in the shadows.

'I'm quite sure Cathy would like to go.' It was the first time he had used her Christian name and Lucía glanced sharply in his direction. 'I have no doubt about Teresa,' he added drily.

'Why can't we all go?' Teresa suggested. 'We could ride over with Manuel in the morning and you and Ramón could bring the car down in the afternoon. That way you wouldn't have to spend a whole day away from Soria,' she added pointedly.

'How about you, Ramón?' Alex asked. 'Will you come?'

He hesitated.

'I've seen *fiesta* many times.'

'It is never twice the same,' Alex reminded him, looking directly into his troubled eyes.

'I can't promise.'

'You will be at the *puerto*,' she said confidently, 'so why don't you join us at Orotava for a meal?'

He drew a deep breath.

'Why not?' he said. 'There is no reason why I shouldn't.'

'None at all,' Alex assured him. 'And now I really must be off or it will be dark before I get home.'

'Which means your headlights still don't function,' Ramón grinned.

'I've had them attended to,' Alex smiled, 'but they're still unreliable.'

'What you need is a new car!'

'I'm afraid so.' Alex picked up her shoulder-bag. 'Nobody must opt out of the *fiesta*,' she warned, her smile embracing them all. 'Not even you, Lucía!'

'*Fiestas* don't interest me any more,' Lucía declared, moving along the terrace to speed her on her way, 'but this time I will come.'

She stood beside the white two-seater while Don Jaime opened the door on the driver's side for Alex to get in, very much the gracious hostess bidding a safe journey to the departing guest. She won't let go, Catherine thought. Lucía will never let go. If Don Jaime doesn't marry her she'll find some other way of remaining in command at Soria, whatever it might cost in heartache to others.

For the next few days Lucía seemed to be constantly in the background whenever Don Jaime was in the house. Ramón she could trust in Catherine's company, but not her senior brother-in-law, although it seemed that he had few interests beyond the estate. He worked hard from early morning till nightfall, and after that he shut himself in his study with a mound of paper-work which seemed to grow higher every day.

'What Jaime needs is an efficient secretary,' said Teresa,

'but I doubt if he would let me help. He declares that my writing is illegible and I can't type, but I could go through the mail for him.'

'Why don't you suggest it?' Catherine asked.

'I have, but he seemes to think I would be better employed with my schoolwork. He's got this thing about education, you see, wanting me to be a regular "bluestocking", as you say in your country.'

'Not only in my country,' Catherine laughed, 'but I agree with your uncle, up to a point.'

'It seems ridiculous calling Jaime my uncle,' Teresa mused. 'He is only a dozen years older than I am.'

'Which is quite a bit. And you told me that Lucía is . . .?'

'Twenty-nine,' Teresa whispered in a hollow voice. 'Soon she will be thirty.'

'How terrible!' Catherine teased.

'Now you are laughing at me,' Teresa returned, 'but you can mock all you like. I know she hates to be older than Jaime, though it is only by a year. Spanish women age more quickly,' she added speculatively, looking closely at Catherine, 'but they are more worldly-wise than English girls once they have been married.'

The married state was something that Lucía had greatly prized, and Catherine was quick to recognise the fact, although she could not discuss it with Teresa. Almost every day since their arrival stepdaughter and stepmother had come to verbal blows on one issue or another, and because she was the older in experience Lucía had generally won the argument. Some of their battles were over such trivial things that Catherine felt impatient with them both, but she reminded herself that she was not well enough established at Soria to interfere in these matters. She might try by mild suggestion to influence Teresa, but she could not confront Lucía on her stepdaughter's behalf.

'Perhaps it would be easier if you didn't always address her as *madrastra*,' she suggested. 'Nobody likes to be constantly reminded that they're second best.'

Teresa turned round in a fury.

'She is not my mother!' she cried. 'Why should I call her that? My mother was good and sweet and *delicada*. She died when I was very young.'

'But you remember her?'

Teresa hesitated.

'Why should I not?' she protested. 'I remember how kind she was and really beautiful. She wasn't tall, like Lucía; she was small, like me. Small, with black hair. There is a portrait of her in the study, where Lucía seldom goes.'

Don Jaime seemed determined to keep the memory of her mother alive, whatever Lucía might think. Everything else which might have belonged to Eduardo's first wife had been removed from view, but the portrait might have been hung in the study by Eduardo himself before his death and Don Jaime had kept it hanging there. He would not have it banished to a store-room or destroyed altogether.

How could she possibly guess at the emotions of these people she had come to work with? Catherine wondered. How could she ever hope to understand the fundamental desires they cherished?

Teresa decided to sulk for the remainder of the morning, declaring that she wanted to ride out on her own for a change.

'I never get a chance to gallop when you are with me,' she informed Catherine with the deliberate intention to hurt which made her sound ominously like her stepmother. 'We just keep plodding along.'

'You will take Manuel with you?' Catherine asked.

Teresa drew herself up to her ridiculously small height.

'I have no need of you or Manuel to watch over me,' she said rudely. 'I can look after myself.'

'I hope you can,' said Catherine. 'Where will you go?'

'I have not yet made up my mind.' Teresa kicked at the stone pavement with her kid riding-boot. 'To Las Rosas, perhaps, or San Juan. It is accepted,' she added quickly when she saw the protest in Catherine's eyes. 'I have been there many times.'

San Juan de la Rambla was some distance along the high

coastal road, Catherine had observed from frequent reference to her map, but she could not challenge that pointed 'it is accepted' with which Teresa had sought to silence any further argument.

'You are entitled to some time off,' Teresa pointed out in order to justify her decision to go alone, 'and you wouldn't be able to ride all that distance, anyway.'

Earlier Lucía had set off in the car to pay a call on a friend in distant Tacoronte, saying that she would return by four o'clock, but she had not taken Manuel with her this time. He had been left 'in charge of things' in her absence and he looked apprehensive when Teresa announced her intention of riding out alone.

'You will keep to the *hacienda, señorita?*' he begged. 'It is safer there.'

Teresa scowled.

'I may do, Manuel, but it is not for you to advise me. You are not my servant and certainly not my master!'

He flushed, reaching up to catch at the rein she held loosely in her hand.

'You know that I should accompany you,' he said. 'The *señora* wishes it.'

'And the *señorita* does not!' Teresa struck him over the shoulder with her whip. 'Stand back, Manuel, or I will ride you down!'

It was an ugly exhibition of temper which Catherine had not encountered in her own dealings with Teresa, a protest, perhaps, at yet another form of control which she could very well do without. It could also be attributed to the fact that Manuel was her stepmother's adoring servant, someone to whom Lucía's every whim was a command to be obeyed without hesitation, even without thought.

'Go after her, Manuel,' said Catherine when Teresa had galloped off in the direction of the main road. 'Keep her in sight, if you can.'

He looked at her as if in doubt.

'What is it?' she asked impatiently. 'Why don't you go?'

'I take my instructions only from the *señora*,' he said uncertainly. 'She did not say to follow the *señorita* today while you were with her.'

'But I am not with her, Manuel,' Catherine protested. 'That is just the point. She has gone off on her own to Juan de la Rambla or somewhere called Las Rosas.'

'It is a house,' he said, looking surprised. 'It is on the other side of the valley.'

'Who lives there?' Catherine asked sharply.

'Nobody—now,' Manuel answered. 'It was once the home of Don Jaime before he came to the *hacienda* to live.'

'I see. Do you know why Teresa would go there?'

'I do not know, *señorita*. She is in an evil mood and she must fly off into the hills. Sometimes she will go to Las Rosas and sometimes to the gipsy encampment where they dance *flamenco* in the true way. She goes there to watch.'

Dismay surged into Catherine's heart.

'We must find her,' she said, in spite of the fact that Lucía was not present to give him his orders. 'Manuel, you will go with me. Saddle Vivo and your own pony. I'll be ready in five minutes.'

She hurried towards the stairs before he could offer any further protest, mounting them two at a time in her haste and scrambling into Teresa's yellow jodhpurs and a silk shirt in under five minutes, hoping that Manuel would be waiting with the ponies by the time she returned to the *patio*. When she reached it he was nowhere in sight.

Used by now to the mule-like reluctance of the average Spanish servant when he did not wish to obey or thought an order unjustified, she ran through the house in the direction of the stables where Manuel was struggling into his *poncho*.

'You will not need that,' she told him impatiently. 'Have you saddled both ponies?'

'It is better if I follow alone,' he said.

'No,' she protested, 'I must go with you. I should never have let Teresa go off on her own.'

'She will return,' he declared philosophically. 'She does not stay away for long.'

Teresa rushing headlong into the mountains appeared to be an accepted fact among the servants, but suddenly it seemed to be something Catherine had to stop, an act of bravado or petulance which could yet be nipped in the bud if only they could catch up with her. It was something she had to do, not only to save Teresa from Don Jaime's wrath, but to protect herself. It would have to happen like this, she thought. Doña Lucía will say she left me in charge!

They took the main dirt road, going down across the valley to the other side. The sun was very hot on the lower slopes, and dark *barrancos* cut into the mountainside, scarring it deeply to make the going more difficult. Nothing would grow in them until the black volcanic soil became more friable and then they would become rich, cultivated land to add to the wide boundaries of Soria, more acres for a man to survey from the saddle of a white Arab horse.

Almost as if he had made his appearance on the horizon above them, she could see Don Jaime de Berceo Madroza riding along the nearby ridge looking down on his extended kingdom, triumphantly aware that it was his for as long as he lived.

Then, suddenly, she saw that he was really coming towards them, riding the white horse as she had imagined, his black Córdoban hat pulled forward over his eyes to shield them from the sun. He rode leisurely at first, as if he had yet to recognise them, but when he did he dug his heels into the Arab's flanks to cover the remaining distance in a cloud of dust.

'What are you doing here at this time of day?' he demanded, narrowing his eyes against the strong light. 'And where is Teresa? She must be mad to let you ride out in this heat.' He looked beyond them, realising quickly that they were alone. 'Where is she?' he repeated sternly. 'You had come to look for her.'

'I thought Manuel should be with her when she was going so far.' Catherine could tell him nothing but the truth. 'I ride so very slowly, and she wanted to be on her own. Which is no reason why I should have let her go,' she added honestly. 'I'm to blame.'

He swept her apology to one side with a gesture of his whip.

'Do you know where she has gone?' he demanded.

'She spoke about San Juan de la Rambla.'

'I have come from that direction.'

'Then she must have gone to Las Rosas,' Catherine admitted. 'Don Jaime, I'm truly sorry. I'd forgotten about the heat, about not riding until later in the day.'

She knew now why her head was aching and why the dark volcanic soil seemed to shimmer beneath her. Foolishly she had come without a hat or even a scarf to protect her from the midday sun. Don Jaime made a swift calculation, computing the distance between them and the *hacienda*.

'It will have to be Las Rosas,' he decided. 'We are more than half-way there.'

He drew the silk kerchief from his throat, holding it out to her as he spoke to Manuel in rapid Spanish.

'Put it on,' he commanded when she sat, undecided. 'Or would you rather I gave you my hat?'

'No,' she said. 'It would fall down over my eyes!'

He had made her feel as irresponsible as Teresa, yet he did not seem to blame her entirely for the present situation. He sat looking down at her for a moment as she tied the kerchief about her head.

'You would have been better with the hat,' he said. 'The wide Córdoban hat which shelters us from the sun. Sometimes I think it is like a family responsibility, protecting everything in its shade.' He took the pony's rein. 'We will go straight to the house,' he decided, speaking over his shoulder to Manuel. 'Then we will search for Teresa.'

'I will go now,' Manuel offered eagerly.

'No, we will search together.'

They rode to the edge of the ridge, looking down into the *barranco* where there was little to be seen but wicked black rocks and an old lava stream which had burned its way among them. Although she now wore Don Jaime's silk kerchief over her hair, Catherine was conscious of a lightness in her head which made her feel sick, and every cautious movement the little pony made seemed magnified a thousand times, drumming in her ears until she could no longer think clearly. She couldn't afford to slip from Vivo's back, however, although she wished for nothing more than the feel of solid earth under her feet and the chance to prove that the world was not upended and spinning about her.

Don Jaime came to ride beside her.

'Cathy, are you feeling ill?' he demanded.

'No,' she lied. 'No, I can go on.'

He looked beyond her, calculating distance, and then his eyes narrowed.

'I've a fair idea where we might find her,' he said. 'It isn't very far and it's on our way to Las Rosas.'

They saw the encampment from the top of the next ridge. In a natural hollow in the mountainside, sheltered by a group of stunted trees, several gipsy caravans had been parked by the side of the narrow road. They had been placed strategically in a rough semi-circle, leaving the road and a shallow stream open to access, and in the centre a fire burned, the white wood-smoke rising straight into the windless air.

Grouped around the fire or sprawling on the wooden steps of their vans, the gipsies were enjoying the added warmth of the sun and the impassioned dancing of the younger members of the community whose wild gyrations were inspired by a dark-skinned youth with a guitar.

Don Jaime's jaw tightened in anger, and then Catherine became aware of a horse and rider on the far side of the camp-fire. Teresa was still mounted on her pony, looking more like an equestrian statue carved from stone than any flesh-and-blood creature as she watched the quick heel movements and hand gestures of the gipsy dancers. Oblivious of everything but the music and the fiery execution of *flamenco*, she gazed down at the gipsies, although she made no immediate attempt to join them. If she had done so they would probably have melted away in confusion, shyly suspicious in the presence of a stranger. Unless she had been here before and they were now her friends!

The music ceased and Don Jaime urged the white Arab forward, riding round the edge of the encampment until he came to where Teresa stood, and almost reluctantly Catherine followed, with Manuel bringing up the rear.

As they reached the grassy bank which Teresa had used for her grandstand view she was almost in tears.

'Now you have spoiled everything!' she cried. 'Why do you follow me? I am not in any trouble. All I want to do is watch these people who dance like no one else.'

Don Jaime got down from the saddle, slipping the Arab's rein over his arm as he approached her, and there was no longer any sign of anger in his face.

'Come home, Teresa,' he said quietly.

Teresa's dark eyes filled with tears.

'I would have returned eventually,' she said, allowing him to lead her pony back on to the path.

When she came nearer she looked at Catherine with the faintest of smiles curving her lips.

'I should have taken you with me,' she said, 'then there wouldn't have been all this fuss.'

Catherine tried to smile in return, but the vision she had of Teresa and the pony was suddenly blurred. The ball of the sun seemed to spin round in the sky, its long rays slanting crazily towards her as she heard Don Jaime's familiar voice.

'Let go the rein and leave everything to me.'

She obeyed him automatically, and after that his orders seemed to reach her from some vague distance into which he had evaporated in the light of the sun. She felt her feet touch firm ground, but almost immediately she was lifted again into the saddle. Another saddle, she realised, conscious of her greater distance from the ground. She was sitting high on the Arab's back. The big horse pawed the ground in a spirited desire to move on, but Don Jaime checked it as he gave his instructions to their companions. Catherine heard Manuel say: *'Sí, señor!'* and knew that Teresa had come to put a reassuring hand on her arm, and then Jaime vaulted into the saddle behind her and took up the rein.

'We must get her to Las Rosas,' he said. 'It is the only way. To ride back to the *hacienda* before she is rested would be madness.'

Catherine had passed beyond argument, even if it did seem that he might not want them at Las Rosas, which had once been his home. Her head was throbbing now with a red-hot intensity and only his arm about her kept her upright. She leaned back against him, conscious of the hard, taut body beneath the silk shirt and the firm muscles along his arm. Here was sanctuary when she most needed it; here was security and an untold peace. That was all she was going to think about.

The journey down the other side of the ridge was only a blurred memory by the time they finally reached Las Rosas. The little house stood in a grove of eucalyptus trees, their pungent scent rising into the still air as they approached, and Catherine was lazily aware of yellow stucco walls and grilled windows in the Moorish style and a roof of rose-red tiles. It was a small house but perfectly proportioned, looking down across its unkempt terracing to the sea.

From somewhere beyond the overgrown garden a stout figure in rusty black came to inspect them.

'Ah, María!' said Don Jaime. 'We are in trouble. We have come to shelter from the sun.'

A flood of rapid Spanish greeted his announcement, interlaced by María's toothless smile. She was a very old woman and spoke a patois which only Manuel and Don Jaime could understand, but there was no doubt about her welcome. Rapidly beckoning to an even older man who had hobbled in her wake as far as the gable end of the house, she rushed on ahead of them to chase a gaggle of geese away from the door. Several brown goats had gathered at a respectful distance to study them, their velvet ears pricked in surprise.

'They're not used to intruders,' Don Jaime said as the man chased them off into the surrounding scrub.

And neither are you, Catherine thought vaguely. This is the place where you come to be alone when the intrigues of Soria become too much for you.

As he lifted her down from the saddle his hands were curiously gentle.

'Can you walk?' he asked.

'Yes—of course.'

He led her towards an arched doorway where the old woman stood waiting. She had long, bedraggled hair and rough hands from grubbing around in the soil, but she had the kindest eyes Catherine had ever seen.

'Take care of her, María,' Jaime said.

Beyond the door a dim, cool passageway seemed to stretch into infinity with shuttered windows on either side which shut out the torture of the sun. There was very little furniture, but the tessellated floor was highly polished, making it shimmer like a lake. Catherine stood quite still on the threshold of Las Rosas, drowned in the relief of shade and conscious of a warmth that she had yet to find at Soria.

'*Muchas gracias,*' she said, allowing the old woman to lead her forward.

Don Jaime came up behind them, issuing a string of rapid orders which María hastened to obey.

'Sit down, Cathy,' he said when they reached the long room at the end of the passage. 'You will soon recover now that you are in the shade. It is a discomfort that passes quickly, you will see.'

She could have wept at his kindness when he had every right to be angry.

'Don't blame Teresa too much,' she managed in a shaken whisper. 'She didn't mean to cause—all this upheaval.' She glanced about her, realising that what furniture there was in the room was shrouded in blue-and-white dust covers. 'I'm quite ready to go back to Soria.'

'I think not,' he decided, looking at his watch. 'You will

lie down for an hour and then we shall see about your return. If need be, you can stay here overnight, with Teresa to keep you company.'

'There's no need,' she protested, although her head still ached and her mouth felt dry. 'If I could have something to drink——'

Her voice trailed away and, suddenly, she was swaying on her feet. Don Jaime lifted her in his arms as if she were a baby, carrying her purposefully from the room and down another passageway where María was waiting at an open door.

'In here, *señorito*,' she said. 'It is the room I always keep ready for you.'

She must have known Don Jaime from infancy to have used the diminutive title so naturally, and it spoke of deep affection and pride.

Lying on Don Jaime's bed with her eyes closed, Catherine allowed the world to pass her by. She was vaguely aware of the old woman moving about the room and of Teresa coming to stand beside her for a moment, and then she knew that Don Jaime had returned.

'Drink this,' he commanded, putting strong fingers across her brow. 'It is something to make you sleep for a while.'

Vaguely she wondered what time it was—how long they had taken to reach the gipsy encampment and come on to Las Rosas—and then she drank the cool, clear liquid he had poured into a glass for her and went to sleep.

The light had faded when she opened her eyes again and gradually she realised that the peace of Las Rosas had been rudely shattered. Outside the window a woman's high-pitched voice was raised in angry complaint, and it did not take her long to realise that it was Lucía. Teresa's stepmother had come in search of them.

Dazedly she struggled to her feet, glad that her head had stopped aching and her limbs were now her own, although she had to support herself by holding on to one of the high, carved posts at the foot of the bed for a moment before she could cross the floor.

'You are to blame,' Lucía was saying. 'You encourage her!'

She could not hear Don Jaime's reply, but it seemed that Teresa had dissolved into a flood of tears.

'Crying is of little use,' Lucía told her, 'but perhaps you thought you could stay here, away from my influence. Well, now you know better. You will ride to Soria with Manuel before the light fails and you will send the car back here for your irresponsible tutoress, who will now have to go!'

The elation in the last few words was unmistakable, and Catherine stood tensed, listening for Don Jaime's reply.

'We must wait till we have calmed down before we make any decisions,' he said. 'I do not consider this entirely Cathy's fault. It was an accumulation of circumstances which unfortunately went wrong. When we get back to Soria we will discuss it.'

The finality of his decision was something which Lucía could do nothing about. She came to stand in the bedroom doorway while Catherine brushed her hair into place.

'You understand, of course, that you will be held responsible for this—insurgency,' she announced. 'You knew quite well that you were not to ride outside the *hacienda*, whatever Teresa decided to do. She is not to be trusted. She is wild and wayward and ready to take any risk, but you should have known better. My brother-in-law has sufficient responsibility to shoulder without you adding to it by fainting from heat on his doorstep.'

Catherine turned from the mirror to face her.

'I did my best, *señora*,' she said quietly. 'I followed Teresa as quickly as I could and I didn't ask to have sunstroke.'

'No, indeed,' Lucía agreed. 'You look terrible, but I think you are ready to travel the short distance back to Soria by car. There can be no question of your riding back,' she added, 'even if Don Jaime was foolish enough to bring you here on his own horse.'

She knew so much that Catherine could only assume that she had questioned Manuel, who was her obedient servant.

As she stood framed in the doorway dressed in her conventional outfit of white breeches, white silk shirt and black riding-boots, with her wide-brimmed black hat slung over her shoulders, she was a commanding figure, not beautiful but certainly distinctive and with an unmistakable air of authority that chilled Catherine into silence.

'Some food is being prepared for us,' she said, 'at considerable inconvenience. Las Rosas is no longer occupied, since both Ramón and Don Jaime live at Soria at the moment. Should either of them marry, naturally the other would move to Las Rosas. That is why María and her husband are kept in employment, to look after the house and see that it is aired. They are too old to do a good job, but Jaime insists that they should stay. They live in a *cabaña* further down the hill.'

Catherine moved towards the door.

'I am ready now,' she said. 'I won't keep you waiting.'

Lucía made no effort to move away. She had effectively blocked the doorway and she stood looking at Catherine with ice-cold eyes.

'I think you should know that it is only a matter of weeks before Don Jaime and I will be announcing our engagement,' she said. 'It is something we have kept to ourselves because of Teresa who, of course, will not approve. You do not say anything, Miss Royce,' she went on. 'Is it because you are so surprised or because you had aspirations of your own, even after so short a stay at Soria?'

Catherine, who had been shaken by the unexpected announcement, looked back at her in disbelief, thinking about Manuel and that clandestine meeting on the moonlit terrace no more than a week ago.

'You do not credit what I say?' Lucía came a little nearer. 'But that is foolish, since I could dismiss you on the spot. You are only here to teach my stepdaughter, not to fall in love with every man who may look your way.'

'I am not in love——'

'Already you are doubtful about it?' Lucía's gloved hands were suddenly clenched on the whip she carried. 'You would be very foolish, Miss Royce, to set your sights too high. Of course,' she added, 'if you were to tell me that it is Ramón who has taken your fancy I would understand. He makes himself deliberately attractive to everyone.'

Catherine drew in a deep breath.

'Aren't we being just a little ridiculous?' she suggested. 'I have been here so short a time, as you have just pointed out, that I could not possibly have fallen in love with any-one.'

Lucía's brilliant white teeth flashed in a mocking smile.

'How truly English!' she exclaimed. 'No doubt it is your way to measure love or passion by time, but who is to say when we fall in love, Miss Royce, or how long it takes? One day—two, or half a lifetime. You are inexperienced in these things, I see, but I have given you a warning. I will not allow you to stay at Soria if you do not concentrate on your work and forget about falling in love. Yes, I will see that you leave the *haçienda* before you cause any damage in our lives!'

Malice and determination struggled in her eyes as she turned away, and Catherine stood in the darkening bed-room when she had gone, wondering what would happen now. She had been employed by Don Jaime and his grand-mother to teach Teresa, and the Marquesa, at least, had accepted her with warmth, but how could she remain at Soria in the face of Lucía's evident disapproval? In a few weeks, Lucía had said, she would announce her engagement to her brother-in-law and after that she would be in supreme command, as she had been when Eduardo was alive. Mistress of Soria again!

With so much ambition in her heart, did it matter whether Lucía loved Jaime or not? Did it even matter about Manuel who could so easily be sent away? Lucía would dis-miss her lover with as little thought as she would give to any other servant who had ceased to please her.

It was all wrong! Catherine turned back into the room where she had slept so peacefully for the past two hours, thinking how clearly it reflected the personality of its owner. Jaime was so forthright, so honest in every way, and Lucía had no right to trick him in any way, Lucía and Manuel, who could not help being in love with a ruthless mistress who wanted nothing but power. But perhaps it was the Spanish way—a little romance here and there, a little loving to pass away the warmth of a summer's afternoon!

She shrank from the suggestion, knowing how wrong she could be in Don Jaime's case. He was not the man to love lightly and perhaps not for a second time. Alex Bonnington had spoken about 'twisting a knife in an old wound' when she had been discussing mistakes, and he had admitted to the folly of youth and love. If he had loved in his youth it would have been deeply, she felt sure, and suddenly her heart contracted with an almost unendurable pain. 'Don't love him!' reason cried deep within her, but she knew that reason had nothing to do with love. Already Don Jaime de Berceo Madroza had stretched out a *conquistador*'s hand and touched her susceptible heart.

A meal had been set out for them in the kitchen where it had been hastily prepared, the big yellow chick beans heaped in an earthenware bowl in the centre of the table and served with morsels of boiled beef and chicken and scraps of bacon.

'*Cocido!*' Teresa exclaimed, preparing to eat her fill. 'I haven't tasted it for ages.'

Catherine sat on the wooden bench beside her, unable to eat but grateful for the wine which María had produced from a large stone jug. It was rough and cool, the produce of Soria's own vines, perhaps, but certainly local.

'Don't drink too much of that,' Don Jaime advised, coming to sit down beside her. 'It's fairly potent when it has lain for a while. How do you feel now?' he asked.

'Very much better, thanks to you.'

'Well enough to return to Soria?'

Their eyes met.

'Quite well enough.'

She could not fail to see the look of satisfaction in his eyes as he rose to his feet, thinking how right she had been about his not wanting them at Las Rosas. It had been a necessary invasion, but he would be relieved when they finally departed.

Teresa and Manuel had both disappeared immediately after they had finished their coffee, but Lucía had tethered her black horse firmly to the fence which surrounded the courtyard, determined to stay where she was until the car arrived. The atmosphere in the tiny kitchen became electric even with the homely figure of María hovering around as she cleared up the remnants of their meal. Don Jaime drank the remainder of his wine and went out.

'You and Teresa have cost him half a day's work between you,' Lucía pointed out. 'You do not seem to understand how busy he is at this time of year. The *hacienda* does not run itself, Miss Royce, and he can hardly be grateful to you for adding to his burdens instead of lightening them. Of course, he should have dealt firmly with the whole problem of your age at the beginning, in Madrid.'

'Perhaps he should,' Catherine agreed faintly, 'but he didn't because I may have talked him into believing in me.'

'And the Marquesa would have helped you,' Lucía observed, her mouth twisting in a sneer. 'When she comes to stay here there is always trouble, and even when she is far away in Andalusia she exerts her authority where Teresa is concerned. You would not like to be a stepmother, Miss Royce, I can assure you, and I am too young for the rôle. Teresa has defied me ever since I married her father four years ago. She was twelve then, but amazingly precocious, even for a Spanish child. Eduardo and Jaime had spoiled her between them and Ramón was too near her own age to be anything but a daring playmate. That was the situation I had to tackle at Soria when I came here as Eduardo's bride. Not a particularly romantic one, you will agree.'

'I'm sure you had the—strength of purpose to handle it in your own way,' Catherine answered. 'The tragedy seems to be that—your husband died so soon afterwards.'

'Less than a year afterwards.' Lucía's expression had not changed, even at the mention of her loss. 'There was much to do for Soria, and Jaime and I did it together. Eduardo had allowed the estate to deteriorate at an alarming rate after his first wife absconded to South America to resume her dancing career. There was no other man, you understand; just her career.'

Stunned into silence by the unexpected revelation, Catherine stared at her incredulously.

'You are surprised that I should tell you all this,' Lucía suggested, 'but it is best that you should know the truth about Soria. Eduardo destroyed it by continuing neglect while Jaime had to look on, unable to do anything much about it because there was so little money to spare. That's where I came in,' she added proudly. 'I had the money they needed. I knew Eduardo was fond of me, of course, in a second-best sort of way, but it was really Soria that mattered most.'

'It must have been—difficult for you in the beginning,' Catherine acknowledged.

Lucía smiled.

'Oh, don't feel sorry for me, Miss Royce,' she said. 'I am—how do you say?—a realist. I do not expect too much from life or love, but what I have built up at Soria is mine. I will not allow anyone to take it from me.'

'Surely it will all be yours when you marry Don Jaime,' Catherine said heavily.

'Sí, that is so!' Lucía was still studying her closely. 'He does not know that I have spoken to you in this way, you understand?'

'Certainly.'

A heavy silence descended on the kitchen as María went out with the scraps of left-over food for the goats.

'What will you do when you leave Tenerife?' Lucía asked, breaking it to put the question she had been determined to ask.

Catherine had not even thought about the future, even when Lucía had first threatened her with dismissal.

'Go home,' she said. 'Back to London, where I suppose I really belong.'

A shadow darkened the doorway, but it was Don Jaime who came in and not María.

'Are you ready?' he asked. 'I have brought round the horses.' He was looking directly at Lucía. 'Shall I lead yours so that you can go back in the car?'

'Certainly not!' Lucía straightened the silk knot at her throat. 'I will ride back with you, Jaime. We have much to discuss.'

The car drove into the tiny courtyard, its headlights already on. Catherine could see Ramón behind the steering-wheel with Manuel sitting beside him. Lucía flicked her riding-whip impatiently.

'You had no need to return,' she said as her servant came towards them. 'Why did you disobey my instructions?'

'I came to ride the *señorita*'s pony, *señora*,' he explained, his dark eyes glowing with a reproachful flame. 'You did not give me any special order when you sent me away.'

'All right, Manuel,' said Don Jaime. 'You can ride back with us. No damage has been done.'

Had it not? All Catherine could see in that moment was the anguish in Manuel's eyes as he turned abruptly away to find the pony and lead it back to Soria.

'I'm causing you a lot of trouble,' she apologised as Don Jaime helped her into the car. 'You were busy on the estate.'

'Jaime is always busy,' Ramón assured her, leaning on the steering-wheel, 'but he will make up for it with an early start tomorrow. The light has now gone, so there is nothing we can do in the fields.'

Lucía got into the saddle, reining in the big black horse.

'Diablo will kill her one of these days if she isn't careful,' Ramón mused. 'He's far too powerful for her, but she prides herself on being the best horsewoman between here and Santiago del Teide. She has ridden since she was a child, but then you either are a horse-lover or you are not. We cannot all be budding champions. How are you coming on, by the way?'

'Not very well, as you can see,' Catherine grimaced. 'My

lack of ability was probably the cause of today's little trouble when Teresa wished to gallop for a change.'

'To get something out of her system, I expect.' He put the car into second gear. 'What was it this time?'

'I'm not quite sure.' Catherine was reluctant to discuss Teresa's moods with Ramón, although he probably understood them better than anyone else. 'We had been talking about her mother.'

'Ah!' said Ramón quietly. 'That is a moot point. No one speaks about Carla nowadays.'

'Did you know her?'

'Hardly. I was in Madrid being educated most of the time, and before that I suppose I accepted her as just the most beautiful person I had ever seen.'

'Teresa said how beautiful she was.'

'How can she remember? She was very young when Carla died.'

They drove on in a lengthening silence, bumping over the hard dirt road in the peculiar pale grey light which was all that remained of the blazing day. The sun had gone down like an orange fire-ball, plunging behind the mountains into the sea, and the aftermath had been short and dramatic, a flare of vermilion spreading across the sky to trap the high pinnacles surrounding El Teide in brilliant flame for a moment before it faded as swiftly as it had come.

Before it was dark enough for the first stars to show through they were above the *barranco* and turning along the main road, and Catherine allowed her thoughts to stray to the two figures on horseback they had last seen riding up from Las Rosas, one as tall as the other, both straight in the saddle, riding side by side, one on a white Arab horse, the other on the big black stallion Ramón had called Diablo. They were so much a part of the strange, wild land of deep ravines and rugged mountains that it seemed almost inevitable they should marry and continue to administer Soria together.

'You look sad all of a sudden,' Ramón remarked. 'Do

you still feel light-headed from riding too long in the sun?'

'That must be it.' She gave him a quick smile. 'It was foolish of me to go out without a hat, but it didn't seem important at the time. I love to feel the wind in my hair.'

He took one hand from the wheel to place it over hers.

'You are very sweet, *chiquita*,' he said softly. 'I hope you will stay at Soria for a long time.'

'To amuse you, Ramón?'

'To make my life worth living again!'

'You're absurd!' She moved her hand away.

'Why is it foolish to tell you how beautiful you are and how my heart beats twice as fast when I look at you?'

'Because I think you've said that so often in the past.'

'You are cruel,' he declared, 'and you do not understand me. Even when I play for you with all my heart, you laugh at me!'

'Not *at* you, Ramón, *with* you! There's a great difference.'

'*Yo comprendo!* It is a good thing, is it not, to laugh together and be happy?'

'Exactly!' They had turned in at the open door in the *hacienda* wall. 'Will you go to the *fiesta* with us? You seemed undecided.'

'I was not sure about Orotava,' he admitted, 'but now I will go since Alex has asked me. A year ago we were very close friends, but it came unstuck,' he added in the English idiom which always seemed so incongruous when he used it, with typical Spanish gusto. 'We are no longer of one mind.'

'Alex is a very understanding person, I should think.'

'I agree.' He thought for a moment. 'But she is settled in her ways.'

'Meaning that she doesn't tilt at every windmill she comes across?'

He laughed spontaneously.

'Like Don Quixote! You think that is me? You think that I go out seeking adventure for adventure's sake?'

'Don't you?'

He shrugged.

'Not always. I know what I really want to do, and when I am no longer needed at Soria I will do it.'

'You will go to Madrid?'

'Why not? You must see that there is nothing for me here.'

'Even if Don Jaime still needed you?'

'He will not need me so much when there is no debt to pay back to Lucía.'

'You mean—when they are married?'

'He will pay off the debt before then. He would not marry in order to cancel it, you understand?'

'I think so.' They had reached the house. 'Teresa has not come home yet.'

'She will come soon. We did not pass her on the road,' Ramón explained, 'because there is a shorter way through the plantations and she would take that.'

The house seemed deserted, although lights were burning in the kitchen section overlooking the stable yard. Ramón pulled the car up at the end of the terrace, waiting in silence for her to get out.

'Cathy,' he said, bending over the steering-wheel to look at her, 'whatever you think of the present situation—of Lucía and Jaime—stay at Soria for Teresa's sake—and mine.'

She stood for a moment without answering him.

'It will not be my decision,' she said, at last. 'How can I stay if I'm finally asked to go?'

Before he could answer Teresa made her appearance at the far end of the *patio*, followed by Alfredo.

'You beat me to it!' she exclaimed. 'So much for my shortcut.' She tossed her rein to the waiting Alfredo as she dismounted. 'Lucía would ride back with Jaime, of course.'

'They left Las Rosas as we drove away,' Ramón told her. 'Soon they will join us.'

'Not me,' said Teresa. 'I'm tired and will go to bed.'

'Without your dinner?'

'I ate well at Las Rosas.'

Ramón did not try to hide his amusement.

'I can imagine!' he said. 'Do you wish me to convey your regrets to Lucía?'

'If you wish, but it will be of no consequence either way. *Buenas noches*, Cathy. *Lo siento mucho!*'

'Teresa apologises so prettily,' said Ramón. 'She could get away with murder if she felt like it.'

'You're ridiculous!' Catherine smiled.

'You know I speak the truth,' Ramón protested. 'Already you have forgiven her for causing such trouble this afternoon because she has made her pretty apologies.' He got out of the car to stand beside her in the *patio* where the shadows were deep. 'You would never hold a grudge, would you?' he said, putting his arm about her. 'You would always be generous.'

He stooped to kiss her on the cheek, but she backed away.

'No, Ramón,' she said. 'Not tonight! I'm in no mood for a serenade in any key.'

He laughed softly in the darkness.

'I will come and play for you later on,' he promised. 'Under your window.'

'I'll be sound asleep.'

'I told you that you were cruel!' He sighed heavily as the sound of horses' hooves reached them from the approach to the stable yard. 'It is Lucía, come home with Jaime.'

He did not move away as the two figures came along the terrace and Catherine felt the deep colour of embarrassment staining her cheeks as Don Jaime recognised them. Lucía, in her turn, seemed faintly amused.

'Where is Teresa?' she asked. 'I must go in search of her.'

Ramón moved from Catherine's side as his brother switched on the wall sconces to flood the hall with revealing light.

'You must be tired,' Jaime said to Catherine. 'Go to bed

and some food will be sent up to your room. I will speak with you in the morning.'

His voice had been cool with disapproval, although he had been solicitous for her wellbeing because she had felt so ill at Las Rosas, and to Catherine it seemed ominous that he should wish to speak with her privately in the morning. The prospect of instant dismissal was suddenly bleak.

'If you will give me a few minutes to change,' she offered proudly, 'I'm quite well enough to listen to what you have to say.'

Some of the anger had gone out of his eyes, but he said almost indifferently:

'The morning will do, Cathy. I have a buyer coming at eleven o'clock. If you can come to the study at ten I will not keep you long.'

CHAPTER FIVE

At ten o'clock the following morning Catherine went briskly across the hall and tapped on the study door.

'*Adelante!*'

She took a deep breath and went in.

Don Jaime was seated at an enormous black desk in the centre of the room, but he rose to his feet as she entered, pulling forward a chair for her to sit down.

'How do you feel?' he asked.

'Completely recovered.' Should she apologise for the events of the day before or leave him to reprimand her in his own way? 'I never thought I would sleep so soundly.'

'You were exhausted. It was a long way for you to ride in the sun. Remember never to go out again without a hat. But I think you have learned your lesson in that respect,' he added.

'I'll borrow one from Teresa.'

They were speaking about the future, even though it was in an oblique sort of way, and Catherine had imagined that there was not going to be any future for her at Soria. Her heart lifted a little, although she had tried not to let him see how distressed she was.

'Ah, Teresa!' he said. 'I want to talk to you about Teresa.'

She waited for him to continue, her hands folded on her lap, her eyes clear on his.

'You have already helped her in a good many ways,' he said unexpectedly. 'She is no longer as sullen as she was, although she will always be unpredictable. She is too much her mother's daughter, I fear, to change completely, and I would not wish her to be entirely without spirit.'

He looked above her head to where a life-sized portrait

115

in oils hung on the wall above a sofa upholstered in ruby-red velvet.

'You will see what I mean if you are any judge of a painted likeness,' he suggested.

Catherine turned in her chair to look at Carla de Berceo Madroza for the first time. What she saw was a young girl in her late teens with glossy black hair which cascaded over her shoulders to frame a face so hauntingly beautiful that she caught her breath in instant admiration. Carla's skin was like alabaster and the blue eyes, half-hidden by a fringe of black lashes, were deep and intense as they gazed back into hers. Small, delicate-looking hands lay clasped in the folds of a voluminous skirt which spread in tier after tier around her, and close against her throat lay the blood-red ruby which Lucía now wore. Subconsciously she noticed that Carla had posed for her portrait on the velvet-covered sofa which now stood beneath her framed likeness, brought to the study, no doubt, by a man who still remained in love with her.

Eduardo or Jaime? Was that why Don Jaime had never married? Could this be the tragedy which had led to the ugly local rumours on his brother's death?

Looking back at the dark, unfathomable face on the other side of the desk she could not bring herself to see the mark of Cain on Jaime de Berceo Madroza's brow.

'She was lovely!' she heard herself say. 'No wonder Teresa worships her.'

He frowned.

'Teresa didn't really know her,' he said abruptly. 'That is what I want to tell you. She has built up an image of her mother which would be hard to dislodge, even if I wished to do so, but occasionally I am worried by the similarity of their natures. You see, Carla did not die here, at Soria. When her child was three years old she ran away. The quiet life we led on the *hacienda* was too dull for her and she went back to Rio de Janeiro to dance.'

He sat gazing at the portrait which faced him across the room.

'My brother met her in Santa Cruz. She was a dancer on the threshold of fame, but they fell in love and married within the month. Teresa was born a year later, small and dark, like her mother, and with much of Carla's fiery intensity in her veins.'

Lucía had been less generous when she had called it 'gipsy blood'.

'She came of gipsy stock,' Jaime continued almost as if he had read her thoughts, 'and perhaps that is why she danced so well and why she would never have settled at Soria or anywhere else. I dare say she was fond of my brother in her own way, but she loved dancing even more. She saw fame ahead of her and a different way of life, and she abandoned her child and her husband to go in search of it.'

He did not sound like a man who had been deeply in love with his brother's wife. He had been sorry for Carla and Eduardo and little, innocent Teresa at the time, and he had done his best to make amends to Teresa, at least. Only now it seemed that Teresa was prepared to run contrary to all her teaching and to the Marquesa's undoubted love for her. Catherine watched his mouth firm into an implacable line.

'I promised my brother to take care of her,' he said firmly, 'and I owe it to the family to see that no harm comes to her of her own making until she is really able to judge for herself. She will go to Madrid in a year's time to the University to finish her education, and then, if she still wants to dance, she can do so.'

'I think you're being very fair,' Catherine said, although Carla's intense blue gaze seemed to register some sort of protest from the canvas hanging on the wall behind her, 'and I believe in the end Teresa will respond.'

He sat looking at her in silence for a moment.

'I think, in an odd sort of way, that will be up to you,' he said, at last. 'She speaks highly of you, Cathy, even after so short a time, and you are young and progressive enough to understand her. I confess that I did not think you at all suitable when we first met in Madrid—I had quite the wrong idea of what a responsible teacher should look like—but now I am prepared to apologise. I see that what Teresa really needs is a companion, someone near her own age but more mature.'

'I must try to fill the bill, Señor Don Jaime.' She gave him his full title with an impish smile in her eyes because she was so relieved. 'In the end I think Teresa may come to terms with her desire to dance and accept the fact that you are trying to give her the best sort of life possible. Sometimes I feel convinced that she already knows how lucky she is in that respect, but you can't blame her for wanting to kick over the traces occasionally.'

He smiled at that, and she rose, confronted by the litter of papers on the broad desk between them. 'Teresa thought she might be allowed to help you,' she suggested. 'It would be something constructive for her to do.'

Jaime looked at the accumulation of letters and business documents spread out before him.

'She wouldn't stay at it for five minutes,' he predicted. 'She is like Ramón in that respect, too erratic by far.'

'Would you let me help?' she asked impulsively. 'I took a business course after I left school and I can type. When Teresa is at her music lessons I have very little to do.'

He hesitated.

'It wasn't exactly in your contract,' he pointed out.

'Does that matter? I wouldn't expect you to pay me.'

'But that is very unbusinesslike of you,' he said. 'I will give you a salary for what you do. It would be a great help to me,' he acknowledged, 'since I'm not exactly cut out for office work. Being closed in, sitting behind a desk even for an hour or two, irks me.'

'Then it's settled.' It was foolish to feel such childish elation over such a little thing, Catherine told herself. 'Do you wish me to start this afternoon?'

He cast his eyes over the piles of foolscap.

'It's a formidable task,' he observed.

'I'll cope.' She felt almost excited at the prospect. 'I'll deal with the letters first and try to pair them with the relevant documents, and when I'm really stuck I'll come and say so.'

'There's a typewriter somewhere. Eduardo used to use it.' He opened a cupboard door. 'In here, I think. Yes, here we are! Will you be able to manipulate such an ancient machine?'

'I can try.'

'Lucía has used it once or twice, but she considered it inadequate.'

For the first time Catherine thought of Lucía, realising that she had not won the day in her argument with her brother-in-law on the long ride back from Las Rosas.

'I hope Doña Lucía won't think I'm neglecting my duties where Teresa is concerned,' she began uncertainly, but Jaime cut her short.

'Why should she? You were not engaged to instruct Teresa twenty-four hours of the day. I shall tell Lucía what we have arranged.'

Once again he was the autocratic master of Soria, the arbiter of all their fates while they remained under his roof. Catherine could not argue with him nor would Lucía be able to do so unless she had a very strong case to present.

When she told Teresa about the new arrangement her pupil seemed vastly amused.

'Lucía will hate the idea,' she said, 'and so will Ramón.'

'Why Ramón?'

'Because he likes to think that you are there all the time at his beck and call.'

'You exaggerate!'

'No, I know Ramón very well. He is never happy unless he has a pretty girl at his feet.'

'It should be the other way around!' Catherine laughed.

Teresa shook her head.

'Ramón will pretend to fall at your feet, but he will not mean it.'

'I'll remember the warning!'

'Alex Bonnington was the only one who sent him away —how do you say in English?—with a fly in his ear.'

'A *flea*, but I don't think the Marquesa would appreciate the expression!'

'I wish she would come to visit us,' Teresa mused. 'It is never dull at Soria when she is here. Perhaps she will, one of these days, when she grows tired of Andalusia, although I cannot think how long it will take. When are you going to start work for Jaime?'

'This afternoon, when you go for your music lesson.'

Twice a week Teresa made the journey to Santa Cruz to be instructed by a well-known professor of music in the art of playing the piano, and quite often she would accompany Ramón when he took up his guitar in the evening, although there were a good many arguments between them over the finer points of presentation. Ramón, who was self-taught, was unable to read music, but their disputes generally ended in laughter or a compromise, which seemed to please them both.

'I thought you might come with me to Santa Cruz,' Teresa pouted. 'You could look round the shops while I was with the professor and then we could have tea at the Mency or the Bruja, where there is a swimming-pool!'

'Teresa, stop! I've already told you I'm going to work,' Catherine protested. 'If we have a full day off for the *fiesta*, I really should do something constructive to earn my keep.'

Teresa regarded her pensively for a moment.

'You are much too conscientious,' she declared. 'Maybe Lucia will want to go to Santa Cruz.'

The car drove off with Teresa sitting in the back in solitary state, however. It was two o'clock and the noise in the kitchens was beginning to die down. Soon it would be the *siesta* hour and a deep quiet would settle on the house itself to match the peace of the sun-drenched plantations beyond. Now and then a lorry would trundle by, laden with banana fronds, but otherwise there would be little sign of life in the shimmering heat. It would be even warmer in Santa Cruz, where the mountain wind didn't penetrate. Catherine was glad she had stayed at Soria.

At three o'clock she made her way towards the study, opening the door on the confusion which lay within. She crossed to the desk with the odd feeling of being watched, but the only gaze she encountered was the painted one on the wall above the red velvet sofa. Carla de Berceo Madroza looked back at her with pensive eyes. 'What are you doing here?' she seemed to say. 'It is no place for you to be.'

She settled down to work, her gaze drawn again and again to the beautiful, painted face, her eyes fastening on the fabulous ruby at Carla's throat. It was the kind of jewel that only someone like Carla could wear to advantage, she thought, fire and blood imprisoned in a precious stone. Teresa could have worn it, but it was wrong for Lucía, who was too cold to show it off to advantage. It was a gem to reflect the fire in its wearer's eyes, not to lie dormant among the lace at Lucía's throat.

She worked till the clock on the high chimneypiece struck five and by then she had tidied most of Don Jaime's papers into neat piles, ranging them in order of importance along the desk. It had been a gallant effort and she felt pleased with herself, so pleased that she did not hear the door opening.

'What are you doing here, may I ask?'

Lucía's incisive question cut across her pleasant musings like the crack of a whip.

'I've been working.' Catherine rose from the desk. 'I offered to help Don Jaime in my spare time, since he appeared to have so much else to do.'

Lucía came further into the room.

'What do you hope to achieve?' she demanded. 'Do you imagine that working for him will make him appreciate you more? If so you are mistaken. Yesterday you were almost on your way back to England because he thought you careless and inefficient, so you cannot hope to impress him by typing a few letters and clearing up a mess.'

'I like the work,' Catherine said defensively, 'and I had nothing else to do when Teresa was at her music lesson. It was too hot for Santa Cruz in the afternoon.'

'Don't trouble with excuses,' snapped Lucía. 'I know quite well why you are doing this. You imagine that you can make yourself indispensable to him as an unpaid secretary.'

'Not unpaid. He has offered me a fee.'

'Indeed?' A slow, dark colour mounted into Lucía's cheeks. 'And you have accepted it, no doubt.'

'Naturally. Don Jaime pointed out that it was a business arrangement, and it was the easiest way to settle the matter.'

Lucía did not appear to be listening. She had turned round and was looking at the portrait of her predecessor, and all the venom of which she was capable was reflected in her eyes.

'You understand that you are unwelcome here,' she said. 'You have never been anything else than a trial since you came.'

'Yes, I think I realise that now,' Catherine acknowledged, 'but I've done my best, Doña Lucía, hoping to please you.'

'Hoping to please Jaime, you mean! Well, you may do so for a week or two, but it will not last. He has very little faith in women and that is something you cannot change. Even that old woman, his grandmother, has no real power over him.'

'Then I have very little hope,' said Catherine, trying to smile.

Lucía continued to study the portrait, staring at Carla's painted face as if she might find an answer to the unspoken question in her heart.

'I never tried to take her place,' she said, speaking almost to herself. 'I couldn't have done, even if I had wanted to, but I did more for Soria in the end. Jaime is aware of that,' she declared aggressively. 'He knows how much the *hacienda* owes me and he will not overlook it.' She swung round to confront Catherine again. 'You may work your fingers to the bone for him if it pleases you, but he will not forget what he owes to me!'

'I'm sure he wouldn't wish to forget,' said Catherine, feeling that the whole thing was becoming embarrassing. 'He—wants to marry you. I think you said you would be engaged quite soon.'

'Yes! Yes, that is true,' Lucía said emphatically. 'I have full control in this house, you understand, even now?'

As Catherine preceded her to the door the painted eyes of Eduardo de Berceo Madroza's first wife seemed to follow them out.

Teresa was late coming back from Santa Cruz.

'I met someone,' she said mysteriously. 'An old friend of the family.' She flung her leather music-case to one side. 'How exciting it is in a city!' she exclaimed. 'Even in Santa Cruz. We had tea at one of the new hotels on the beach. Where is Lucía?'

'In the kitchens, I think.' Catherine felt slightly uneasy. 'You'd better hop upstairs quickly and change. It's after six o'clock.'

Teresa laughed.

'It would be to no purpose,' she decided. 'Manuel will tell her, anyway. I feel sorry for Manuel, you know,' she went on. 'He is so slavishly devoted to my *madrastra*, yet she cares nothing for him. One day I think he will see how it is and then he will go away to break his heart in secret somewhere else.'

'You talk too much,' said Catherine, moving towards the stairs.

'I see far more than anyone thinks,' Teresa returned positively. 'But tell me what you will wear for *fiesta* tomorrow,' she added lightly. 'Have you any special dress? We must all look really beautiful so that we do not disgrace Don Jaime!'

When she gave her uncle his full title she was generally teasing.

'You do not answer!' she protested, turning at the branch of the stairs. 'Have you nothing to wear?'

'I didn't think I would be going to a *fiesta*.'

'It is only a minor one. Nothing like Corpus Christi, you understand, but everyone wears their prettiest dress and there is dancing in the streets.' Her eyes lit up. 'It can be great fun. You will ride in a carriage, of course, with Alex Bonnington, but I will go on horseback with Ramón and Jaime.'

'And Lucía?' Catherine asked involuntarily.

'I don't know. She rarely goes to *fiesta* and never to a *feria*, but this time I think she will be there.' Teresa gave her a sidelong glance. 'She looks magnificent on horseback, but she will not ride. That would be undignified. Besides,' she added, her face darkening, 'she would not be able to wear my mother's ruby if she went on horseback.'

The ruby was a sore point with Teresa, who coveted it because it had once belonged to her mother. Catherine steered the conversation back to the less dangerous subject of what she should wear for the *fiesta*.

'That pretty dress you had on the other evening,' Teresa suggested, her mood changing dramatically. 'You could dress it up with a brightly-coloured sash. I have many of them in the *baúl* in my room. You must come and choose.'

The ancient leather trunk with its studded corners proved a veritable goldmine to be explored with much enthusiasm.

'You could have this,' Teresa suggested, holding up a beautiful *mantilla* which Catherine had been admiring. 'It will look nice, but it will also keep you warm if the wind blows too strongly. Or this,' she added, running a bright pink sash through her fingers. 'Choose quickly and we will try them on!'

Vividly intense, she was already half-way to the *fiesta*, eyes sparkling, red lips parted in anticipation, her eager feet too impatient to stand still for long, and in that moment she looked really beautiful. She was Carla's daughter all right, wilful and restless as her mother had been even after she had married and borne a child. All the potential dangers were there, mirrored in the dark eyes for anyone to see, but Madroza blood also ran in her veins.

Catherine took a certain amount of comfort from the fact, although she was strongly reminded of Ramón who was determined to take life by the horns in true *torero* style.

She rejected the vivid pink sash in favour of the lovely *mantilla*, unaware that it had been worn by Don Jaime's mother on her wedding day in far-off Andalusia.

'You must dress your hair high and wear a comb,' Teresa declared. 'It holds the *mantilla* in place. Otherwise it will slip down over your forehead and be a nuisance when you dance.'

'*If* I dance!' said Catherine. 'And I haven't enough hair to wear a comb. Not like Lucía.'

Teresa considered the point.

'Perhaps you are right,' she allowed. 'Then you must wear the *mantilla* like a shawl to keep you warm.'

The finer points of their wardrobe settled to her satisfaction, she bundled the other heirlooms back into the leather trunk and closed the lid.

'It was made in Toledo,' she explained, running her fingers over the thick, smooth hide. 'It must be very, very old. Really old things can be amazingly beautiful, don't you think, with all the history of a country caught up in them. Just supposing this trunk had once belonged to a *conquistador* who had travelled all over the world to gain new territories for Spain. Can't you see him, Cathy, riding out on his splendid Arab horse to sail away to the Americas, perhaps, or distant Peru, and always returning to the Court with the gift of new lands for his king and queen?'

Catherine looked down at the trunk, aware that she was seeing Teresa in yet another mood, aware, too, that the image of the valiant *conquistador* had also become her personal image of Don Jaime. He had fought to maintain Soria for the people who lived there, for the family which was now his special responsibility, and if he had won and his quest was nearly over she should be glad.

Folding the lovely *mantilla* over her arm, she walked to her own room where she stood gazing at it for a long time before she laid it over the chair beside the window.

In the morning she was wakened by Teresa complaining that it was raining. El Teide was obliterated and a thin mist hung like a veil over the nearer hills.

'We cannot go!' Teresa moaned. 'At least, not to the *fiesta*!'

'Will it be cancelled?' Catherine asked, sharing her disappointment.

Teresa crossed the bedroom floor to hang out of the window.

'It may just be a little shower,' she decided hastily. 'Manuel is the best one to tell us about the weather conditions. I will go in search of him.'

Perhaps Lucía would put her foot down and forbid the excursion altogether if the rain did not stop, Catherine thought, following her downstairs when she had dressed, but it did seem unfortunate that the weather should have changed so dramatically.

'It will ruin the flower-carpets!' Teresa wailed. 'And I so much wanted you to see them!'

'What did Manuel say about the weather?' Catherine asked.

'I could not find him. He is sulking, perhaps, or he might even have gone away. For good,' Teresa concluded with a dark look in the general direction of the staircase where she expected her stepmother to appear at any moment.

'I thought you said he would drive us to Orotava.'

'Lucía will drive if he does not return, or Ramón. I cannot understand Manuel wanting to stay here, anyway,' Teresa rushed on. 'I would not stay for one minute to be scorned by the person I loved.' She considered the hypothetical situation for a few seconds. 'Perhaps I would try to punish them, but Manuel is too docile for that.'

By eleven o'clock the rain had cleared and El Teide looked down at them from a brightly-washed sky. Teresa's spirits soared in response to the sunshine.

'Now we can dress and prepare to go!' she exclaimed.
'Oh——'

Catherine turned at the sharp expression to find Lucía
descending the black oak staircase and coming towards
them. She looked magnificent dressed simply in palest grey
which suggested that the austere black of her widowhood
had finally been laid aside, and her only ornament was, as
usual, the beautiful unmounted ruby hanging from its short
chain in the hollow of her throat. Her superb height gave
her an added elegance which Catherine envied as she
noticed the lovely tortoiseshell comb thrust into the
coronet of her dark hair.

'Are you not ready?' she demanded. 'It is very bad
manners to be late.'

Teresa said: 'We wondered about the rain, and Manuel
is not here to drive us.'

Lucía's eyes sharpened.

'He must be here! I have spoken to him only this morning. But no matter!' she decided. 'We will go without him.
Ramón will drive us.'

Catherine and Teresa hurried upstairs.

'Don't be long! She's already in a bad mood,' Teresa
whispered.

Catherine followed her downstairs again with the *mantilla* over her arm.

'Where did you get that?' Lucía almost pounced on her.

'Teresa thought I might wear it,' Catherine explained. 'It
seemed just right for my dress, but if you don't think it's
suitable——'

'Of course it is suitable!' Teresa interrupted disdainfully.
'You are only wearing it as a wrap.'

Lucía's eyes were still fixed on the *mantilla*.

'You had no right to give it to anyone,' she pointed out.
'It does not really belong to you.'

'I haven't given it away,' Teresa returned with dignity.
'Cathy knows it is only on loan. It creates a better atmosphere, something that is just right for *fiesta*.'

'It is vulgar to overdress,' Lucía reminded her, touching the discreet comb in her hair. 'That is best left to the *canalla*. I can't imagine Jaime appreciating any flamboyant gestures on our part.'

Catherine wished that she had left the controversial *mantilla* in her room, and then, suddenly, her fingers tightened over its soft folds and she was walking determinedly towards the door.

'It will serve two purposes,' she said. 'To make me feel beautiful and to keep me warm.'

'We'll wait here,' said Teresa, parading along the *patio* like a peacock in her blue dress. 'Let Lucía sort out the problem of who shall drive the car.'

Ten minutes later the big black car came round the end of the house with Ramón at the wheel.

'All aboard!' he grinned cheerfully. 'I've been given leave of absence for the whole day.'

Nothing further was said about Manuel's disappearance until they reached Alex Bonnington's bungalow on the outskirts of Orotava. Built high, it was an old house practically hidden in vines but with a wonderful view right down to the *puerto* which it overlooked. An ancient gardener, who had obviously lost his battle with nature some considerable time ago, waved them into a cleared space at the side of the house as Alex herself appeared through a screen of scarlet bougainvillea.

'Everything is ready,' she declared, smiling her welcome. 'I though we would eat in the garden since the sun has come out again. Lucía,' she added, 'what a beautiful dress! You look superb.'

Lucía permitted herself the faintest of smiles.

'It is one my husband was particularly fond of,' she admitted, fingering the jewel at her throat. 'Eduardo always thought this pale colour enhanced the ruby, but he was perhaps over-dramatic in that respect.'

'I don't know,' said Alex, hastily untying her paint-stained overall to reveal her own scarcely-inspired choice of white shirtwaister and red knitted cardigan. 'It's nice to look distinguished.'

She turned to Ramón, who was getting out of the car.

'Greetings!' he said. 'Was I expected for lunch?'

'You're welcome, whether you were expected or not,' she told him generously. 'Jaime has just phoned, by the way,' she added to the company in general. 'He's booked dinner for this evening at one of the seafront hotels.'

'Where we can dance?' Teresa asked excitedly.

'I expect so. All the hotels will be very full, but he's well known in the *puerto* and would be able to book a table easily enough.'

'Is he coming here for lunch?' Lucía asked.

'He excused himself. He has someone to meet.'

They ate the simple meal Alex had prepared sitting in the shade of a floss-silk tree which shed pale pink petals down on their heads whenever the wind blew. Alex had provided a perfectly-made *paella*, a savoury offering of saffron-flavoured rice mixed with titbits of prawns and flaked fish and tender pieces of *calamares* and small clams, decorated on top with strips of sweet red pimento and green peas. It was served in the shallow iron pan in which it had been cooked, and with it they drank a medium golden wine that seemed to trap all the light of the summer's day.

At four o'clock they made their leisurely way down to the *puerto* where the spirit of carnival had spilled out into the streets and along all the narrow ways between the houses and the grand hotels towards the unspoilt heart of the little port where most of its inhabitants were now gathered. Flowers which had initially formed a lovingly-constructed carpet from the nearby church to the plane-fringed square were now trampled underfoot, but fresher blooms had taken their place on draped carriages where elegant *señoritas* sat in twos and threes flanked by handsome escorts on their mettlesome steeds. Here and there a more intrepid girl rode behind her current beau, laughing and throwing kisses to the crowd. The horses, too, were decorated with carnations and scarlet hibiscus twined in their harness and on the fine leather saddles which seemed to be a feature of the Islands.

Catherine's heart stirred with a wild excitement as she watched, and Ramón's arm went swiftly round her waist.

'Come, dance with me!' he said, whirling her away into the happy throng. 'There's nothing wrong with enjoying yourself!'

They were parted from the others, cut off by the noisy revellers as they danced in the cobbled *plaza*, in and out between the trees, and once Catherine imagined that she saw a familiar figure in a red and green *poncho* sitting at a table on the crowded sidewalk with a glass of *caña* in front of him and a black *sombrero* pulled down over his eyes.

'Manuel?' she asked, and Ramón shrugged indifferently.

'Could be,' he allowed. 'Could be anyone. He should come out from under that hat!'

They laughed, dancing on until presently they came back to where they had started and Don Jaime was waiting with the others. It was almost dark now, with the sun already down beyond El Teide, and Catherine had drawn the *mantilla* over her head. For a full minute Jaime looked at her without speaking, taking in the picture she made.

'You are enjoying yourself?' he asked. 'You have taken to the spirit of *fiesta* very easily.'

'The music has a sort of spell,' she said, looking up at him. 'I feel it very strongly tonight.'

He glanced over her shoulder at his brother.

'Spells can be uneasy things to live with,' he said abruptly. 'Take care that you are not hurt.'

Before she could answer they were whisked away in the throng of dancers. She stretched out her hand to Ramón, but it was Jaime who crushed her fingers in his.

'This sort of thing is inevitable,' he said, his lips close against her hair. 'We should not have been standing on the sidewalk.'

Madly her heart leapt at the half-teasing words, and then

his arm went round her and they were swept away in the dance.

It seemed that they danced for ever, on and on with the sound of music in their ears and the scent of a million trodden flowers rising from the pavements beneath their feet. When it was really dark garlands of little lights twinkled beneath the trees, creating a vivid kaleidoscope of brilliant colour under the stars. There was no way of breaking free from the endless chain of dancers, no way that she wanted to find. Jaime's arm tightened.

'You are tired?' he asked.

'Not in the least.' She looked up at him with a happy smile. 'I could dance like this for ever. It's truly wonderful!'

'To the extrovert Spaniard noise and happiness are different words for the same thing,' he smiled. 'We cannot amuse ourselves without the sound of castanets and the music of a guitar.' The fine edge of the *mantilla* blew against his cheek. 'Have you dressed up to please Ramón or to please yourself?' he demanded, pulling it aside.

'To please myself and perhaps to please you. Someone said you would not approve of an ostentatious display.'

He looked down at her, his eyes burning suddenly in the darkness.

'I am only human,' he said, 'and the *mantilla* is the most romantic headdress in the world!'

Their eyes held and slowly he bent his proud head to press his lips against her mouth in a long, deliberate kiss which seemed to draw all her breath away and stop her heart from beating.

'What is *fiesta* without a kiss?' he said, setting her free at last. 'We have come a long way and we must go back to the *plaza* where the others are waiting.'

Was he thinking of Lucía waiting with fury in her eyes and a burning jealousy in her heart? Catherine clung to his hard fingers as he made a way for her through the crowd, and finally they came to the *plaza* where they had first joined the dance. Teresa and Ramón were missing, but Lucía stood beside Alex, tall and straight and accusing as they finally faced each other in the garish light.

'It is time we made our way to the hotel,' she said without reproach, but the very fact that she had subdued her anger was strangely ominous as they searched the crowd for Teresa and Ramón.

Jaime had chosen one of the smaller hotels on the outskirts of the town with a terrace overlooking the sea where they dined in the open air under a canopy of stars. Their reserved table was set in an alcove and the Union Jack and the Spanish flag made from flower heads were intertwined on the white cloth, a gesture by the management which made Lucía frown. Tossing her evening bag on the table, she managed to disturb most of the British flag.

Catherine could not remember what she ate. She seemed to be still under a spell, but spells were dangerous. Jaime had warned her about that only an hour ago, but it did not keep her from looking at him with love in her eyes.

Of course, she could not expect him to see! The kiss he had pressed against her lips had been as unreal as the glittering garlands of tiny lights which had vied unsuccessfully with the distant stars. It had been a traditional part of *fiesta*, she supposed, given lightly and meant to be taken lightly in return, and it was no use thinking that it was entirely out of character as far as Jaime was concerned because she did not really know him.

Now he was the perfect host, attending to them all in turn, laughing with Alex and Ramón and teasing Teresa in the most lighthearted way. When they danced again on the terrace in the starlight it was a conventional measure to the music of a sophisticated orchestra far removed from the sighing of a native guitar.

At midnight they rose to go, pausing on the terrace for a last look at the sea.

'You have enjoyed yourself?' he asked, coming to stand beside her.

'Very much. It's been the most wonderful experience!'

He stood gazing out across the terrace as if he, too, was reluctant to leave.

'If you look carefully,' he said, 'you can see the shape of the smaller islands, La Palma and Hierro, like ghosts in the distance. Gomera is hidden by the mountains, but they are all worth a visit, La Palma especially. The volcano is still active, but there has not been an eruption for many years. La Caldera is a sleeping giant now, like our own Teide.'

Catherine looked out across the ink-black water of the Atlantic to the little island which seemed suddenly very near, its conical peak just visible against the paler sky. It really wasn't so long ago since La Caldera had burst into flame and molten lava to send a black river of death and destruction flowing down to the sea.

She shivered at the thought.

'You are cold?' He took the *mantilla* from the back of her chair and laid it over her shoulders, his hand touching her bare flesh for a moment of ecstasy before she looked up into Lucía's hostile eyes. 'If you are ready we will go.'

Catherine looked away from the little island on the horizon, thinking of the hidden fire in its turbulent heart which could erupt at any moment to devastate and destroy.

Ramón drove the short distance to Orotava, where Alex set out wine and biscuits to sustain them for the remainder of their journey to Soria.

'I hope you will come and see me whenever you like,' she said when they were ready to go. 'You must have some free time now and then, Cathy, and Manuel could bring you across in the car if you don't want to ride all that way.'

'Cathy has forfeited her free time to work for Jaime,' Teresa said airily. 'He really was snowed under with all that paper-work.'

Alex shot a covert glance in Lucía's direction.

'Well—when you have cleared it up,' she said to Catherine, 'or any time you feel in need of a good chatter!'

'I thought you never gossiped, Alex,' said Lucía, turning

towards them. 'But perhaps it is different with someone of
your own nationality. Miss Royce will not be at Soria for
very long, but she is not a prisoner and I'm sure Jaime
understands that she must have time off. He is quite generous in that respect to all his other employees, as you
know.'

For a moment Alex looked as if she were about to make
some crushing reply, and then she remembered her rôle as
hostess and gave Catherine a reassuring smile instead.

'Remember,' she said as they shook hands. 'Come here
if ever you feel in need of help.'

'You're very kind.' Catherine followed Lucía to the door
where the overpowering scent of frangipani met them as
they walked into the starlit garden. 'I'll come, if I may, even
though I don't need help.'

Ramón was holding the car door open for her to get in.

'Buenas noches, Alex!' he said. 'We've had a wonderful
day.'

Alex smiled in the darkness.

'Perhaps you will come again when there is another
fiesta to attend,' she suggested without emotion. 'Buenas
noches, everyone! Velocidad moderada, Ramón!'

Ramón drove more slowly than usual on the way back
to Soria, as if he intended to spin out the hours of their
happiness against the boredom of the coming days. The
road ahead of them was quite clear of traffic, and on the
higher section, where it ran along the backbone of the
island, they caught glimpses of the distant sea, now illum-
ined by the brilliant light of the moon. It shone on the
Pico de Teide and on the lesser, darker mountains surrounding it, edging the distant coastline with silver, and
here and there between the patches of trees it gleamed on
the tiled roofs of sleeping cottages and on the white stucco
walls of a remote farmhouse whose shutters were closely
barred for the night.

To Catherine it was utter magic. The scent of a thous-
and flowers was still in her nostrils and she felt again the
warmth of a man's strong hand against her cheek. She

could not think of the touch of his lips on her mouth because that was for the secret time when she would be alone, at last.

They passed Jaime at the junction of two roads, a tall, dark figure on a white horse silhouetted against the darker hills, and he acknowledged them with a brief wave of his whip. He had put on a long black cloak for the journey to protect him from the mountain winds and it blew out like dark wings behind him as he urged the Arab to a trot.

'He will not be long behind us,' Lucía reflected. 'It is an easy night for riding when there is so bright a moon.'

Obviously someone else was of the same opinion. A short figure on a pony turned in at the *hacienda* entrance before them.

'It's Manuel,' said Teresa. 'He has been to the *puerto*.'

'Without permission.' Lucía's mouth was grim. 'I will speak to him in the morning.'

In the morning, however, it seemed that Manuel was not to be found.

'He *did* ride in ahead of us last night,' Teresa protested. 'Manuel is easy to recognise when he wears that ridiculous *sombrero*, thinking to disguise himself!'

Catherine was instantly reminded of the small, dark figure sitting at the table in the *plaza* with a glass of *caña* at his elbow, but there didn't seem to be any point in adding her knowledge of Manuel's whereabouts to the general conversation. It was a situation for Lucía to deal with in her own way.

The morning passed quickly enough, with the usual noise and bustle emanating from the kitchens while the food was being prepared, but towards midday the tumult seemed to increase. There were comings and goings and the sound of Lucía's voice raised in anger before the sepulchral quiet of the *siesta* hour finally descended on the *hacienda* once more.

Catherine and Teresa ate a light lunch of shellfish, followed by an assortment of fruits and washed down with a glass of *sangria* to which Teresa was strongly addicted, and

after that they read for an hour stretched out on the cane
lounges on the *patio*, away from the sun. Catherine had encouraged Teresa to read aloud, usually from one of the
books which had been forwarded from England, and they
were half-way through *Wuthering Heights*, which the
younger girl found enthralling.

'Were there really such passionate men and women in
England in those days?' she asked, lifting her dark eyes
from the printed page. 'I thought the average English young
lady was quiet and prim.'

Catherine laughed.

'Not all of them, apparently, but I think the Cathys of
Wuthering Heights were few and far between.'

'She had a strange upbringing,' Teresa reflected. 'Do you
think that makes a difference?'

'Sometimes.'

'She was a heartless creature who would not have made
poor Heathcliff happy, anyway,' Teresa declared. 'Even if
she had married him she would have gone on tormenting
him till he died.'

'It was an ill-starred love in the beginning,' Catherine
admitted. 'In the end it destroyed him.'

'Don't tell me!' Teresa cried. 'I hate to hear the end before I am half-way through.'

'Then you'd better read on. If there's anything you don't
understand you must ask.'

Teresa was still reading at five o'clock when Ramón
came in, followed, surprisingly, by Don Jaime.

'We're going to have a storm,' he said, laying his riding-
crop on the glass-topped table near Catherine's chair. 'It's
been brewing all day.'

They looked up at the copper-coloured clouds beyond
El Teide.

'We could do with some rain,' said Ramón, reaching for
a glass of the dun-coloured liquid which was still in the
carafe on the floor by Teresa's side. 'How you can drink
this Spanish Coca-cola is beyond me!'

'You needn't punish yourself!' Teresa stretched to her

full length on the cane recliner. 'It must be quite warm
by this time, anyway. Jaime will pour us all an aperitif if
we are on our best behaviour.'

Jaime smiled, looking down at Catherine.

'You will take a glass of sherry?' he asked.

She nodded, wondering how long he would stay afterwards. Normally he had plenty to do in and around the
house once the light had failed. He strode off to return
after five minutes with the wine and glasses on a tray.

'The kitchens are in an uproar,' he announced. 'Are we
having company?'

'It's been like that all morning,' Teresa informed him.
'Lucía has been on the warpath.'

He set down the tray.

'Perhaps she will join us for a drink,' he said.

'She will, if you ask,' Teresa returned drily.

'It might prove equally effective if you were to make the
suggestion,' Jaime told her. 'There's such a thing as an
olive branch.'

Teresa flushed.

'I could build a tree-house with the branches I've offered
Lucía,' she declared.

'Another one won't hurt, in that case,' said Jaime, pouring the wine into their glasses.

Teresa rose reluctantly, but before she reached the communicating doors into the hall her stepmother was there.
They stared at each other in silence.

'What's wrong?' Teresa demanded, at last. 'Are you ill?'

Lucía seemed unable to speak for a moment, one hand
clutching the lace at her throat as if she were choking.
Jaime stepped forward to take her by the arm, but she
avoided his touch.

'The ruby,' she said in a hoarse whisper. 'It has gone.'

Ramón jumped to his feet.

'You must be mistaken! You were wearing it yesterday. It
could not have disappeared so suddenly,' he declared. 'You
have misplaced it, perhaps.'

Lucía turned her dark gaze full upon him.

'I do not misplace things so easily,' she said in an amazingly calm voice. 'Especially when it is my most precious possession. Your brother gave it to me when we married and I have treasured it ever since. I wear it constantly.'

Catherine caught a glimpse of Teresa's face. It was ashen.

'It'll turn up,' Ramón said. 'It is bound to turn up. You could have dropped it somewhere—in the garden, perhaps.'

Lucía dismissed his suggestion with a withering smile.

'I do not go around dropping priceless rubies all over the place,' she said. 'No, this has been stolen. There is a thief in our midst.'

She did not look at Catherine, but a swift, bright colour stained her cheeks and Catherine knew that she was being accused.

Jaime made a swift movement towards her.

'Sit down, Lucía,' he commanded. 'We must examine the facts.'

She would not obey him, standing dramatically in the doorway still clutching the lace at her throat.

'When you came in last night did you still have it?' he asked, pouring her a glass of wine which she accepted automatically. 'Think carefully.'

'I wore it all day and I put it away in my jewel-case when I went to my room.'

'And the case?' he asked. 'What did you do with that?'

'What I always do. I left it in the drawer of my dressing-table.'

'Locked?'

'No, I never lock it. Up till now it has not been necessary to lock things away.' She glanced pointedly at Catherine this time. 'Jaime, someone has stolen my ruby and you must discover who it is! I have already questioned the servants.'

His face darkened.

'I would rather you had left that to me,' he said. 'What did you discover?'

'Nothing. I believe they are innocent. Most of them have

worked in this house for many years and are to be trusted. I do not think any of them would take what did not belong to them.'

He put down his glass of wine.

'Leave this to me,' he said. 'If you are sure you have looked everywhere in the house we must search the garden.'

'We can't do that till the morning, and I *know* I haven't made a mistake!' Lucía cried. 'You must believe me when I tell you that I put it safely away last night. I seldom wear it through the day, unless on a very special occasion like our trip to Orotava, but you know I am never without it in the evening. It is the one thing I cherish,' she repeated. 'The memory I have of my husband's generosity. Jaime, you must see that I am devastated by its loss!'

'Of course I understand,' he said, managing to lead her to a chair, at last. 'I will do everything I can to get the ruby back. You can be assured of that.'

'You will do nothing tonight?'

'We will search. Teresa will go with you to your room and empty all the drawers. We must make absolutely certain that it has gone.'

Lucía sipped her wine, a wine as red and full of fire as the ruby she had lost, and Teresa went to stand beside her.

'If you are sure you put it carefully away,' she said, her voice curiously unsteady, 'there isn't much point in searching.'

'I have already said so.' Lucía's hand was trembling so much that she spilled some of her wine on the table as she lifted her glass to her lips. 'I wonder why no one wishes to believe me.'

She looked from Ramón to her stepdaughter and then at Catherine, getting unsteadily to her feet.

'She took it!' she exclaimed, pointing an accusing finger. 'I know she did. No one else would dare!'

'Lucía!' Jaime was by her side in an instant. 'You are hysterical. Catherine wouldn't do such a thing. You are so upset about this you don't really know what you are saying.'

'She does not protest her innocence,' Lucía cried. 'She has nothing to say!'

'Because I can't find any words to answer you,' Catherine said slowly. 'I didn't take your ruby. I'm not a thief, but I can understand how badly you feel. All the same,' she rushed on, 'I must protect myself. Please search my room, someone——'

For the first time she looked at Jaime.

'No,' he said, 'that will not be necessary. We must look elsewhere for our thief, if there is one. Lucía, please go to your room in the meantime. I will ring for Eugénie.'

'I do not need her attentions,' Lucía said proudly, 'but in the morning I think you will search to no avail.'

Having regained her dignity, she swept from the *patio*, leaving them to relax, if they could.

'I'm sorry,' said Jaime, coming to stand beside Catherine. 'Can I ask you to forget such an unworthy outburst?'

Catherine was trembling from head to foot.

'I can't believe it!' she cried. 'I never thought anyone would accuse me of theft, especially here, at Soria.'

'Soria isn't accusing you,' Ramón said, coming to put a comforting arm about her. 'Only Lucía. There's a difference.'

The evening meal was a difficult one. Lucía did not come down for it, preferring to eat alone in her room, while Jaime and Ramón did their best to avoid the topic of the ruby as the servants hovered around the table. When they had gone at last, Ramón was first to break the silence.

'Have you thought about Manuel?' he asked his brother.

'Manuel?' Teresa objected. 'Why would he steal from Lucía, of all people? He was her devoted slave.'

'He has disappeared,' Ramón pointed out.

'But he was here last night. He rode in ahead of us,' Teresa remembered. 'No one could fail to recognise him in that ridiculous *sombrero* he wears when he wants to be aggressively Spanish.'

Jaime looked up for the first time.

'You're certain about this?' he asked.

'Absolutely. He turned towards the stables while we came straight to the house.'

'But no one spoke to him?'

'No, not even Lucía,' Teresa answered cynically. 'But she could have sent him away this morning. She was up earlier than any of us and I heard her going round for her horse. I didn't actually *see* her, but Lucía always rides out early.'

'I can't see the point,' Ramón observed. 'What on earth would Manuel do with a ruby?'

'Sell it,' Teresa suggested promptly. 'It must be worth a lot of money.'

'A small fortune, I shouldn't wonder,' Ramón reflected, 'but how would he get rid of it? He couldn't possibly go in to Santa Cruz and say: "Look, I've got this excellent ruby I want to sell. How much will you give me for it?" He is too well known, and so are we.'

'There are other places, apart from Santa Cruz,' Teresa reminded him, 'but I don't think Manuel has it.'

'He's the obvious suspect at the moment,' Ramón decided.

Jaime had remained silent. It was obvious that their suppositions did not interest him very much, perhaps because he already had a theory of his own.

'We're tilting at windmills,' he said. 'We must not condemn anyone—not even Manuel—before we are quite sure that the ruby has gone.'

'I can't imagine Lucía not knowing where she put it,' Ramón mused, pouring their coffee. 'She guards it like a hawk and it's quite true that she wears it most of the time. That's why I think she is telling the truth when she says it has not been misplaced.'

The first flash of lightning lit up the room as the storm centred on Teide and swept down over the mountains. Catherine jumped to her feet.

'If you don't mind I'll go up to my room,' she said. 'I'm rather tired.'

Jaime escorted her to the foot of the staircase, covering the hand she placed on the carved wooden newel-post with his strong fingers.

'Don't worry too much about this, Cathy,' he said. 'We'll find a solution in the morning. Go to sleep, if you can.'

The kindness in his voice almost unnerved her.

'The storm?' she asked. 'Will it last very long?'

'Not too long. It will be over before morning. I will send Teresa up to you,' he offered.

'No,' she protested, 'she mustn't come if she would rather be with you.'

'Ramón and I will go out later on,' he said. 'We must be sure about the dam. If the water floods over or breaks through a wall it could prove ruinous.'

She stood looking at him for a moment, wanting to say so much, and then she fled up the stairs without saying any of it.

The storm lasted for over an hour, thunder and lightning flashing and rolling round El Teide as if all the furies of the underworld had suddenly been released to spend their wrath on a defenceless world. Each lightning flash seemed brighter than the last, illuminating the garden beneath her for a second to plunge it into even greater darkness when it had passed, and the ensuing thunderclaps came relentlessly nearer until they were just above her head.

'I can't sleep,' said Teresa, coming to stand beside her. 'I hate a storm!'

'Are they always as bad as this?'

'More or less. The blessing is they don't last long. I used to watch them when I was younger and wonder why El Teide was so angry, because it seemed that all the noise and clatter was coming from up there, and then, in the morning, when the sun came up and it was all over, I wondered why I had been so afraid. That old mountain looked so benign in the sunshine, washed clean of his rage. Or, at least, I thought so. Are you very angry with Lucía?' she asked abruptly.

'Angry is hardly the word I would use,' said Catherine.
'I feel—condemned.'

'Because you will be sent away if we can't find the ruby?'

'Because I've been branded as a thief.'

'I know you didn't take it,' said Teresa.

Catherine clenched her fists.

'How can you be so sure?' she demanded. 'You have no
proof of my innocence. Neither has Jaime.'

'He would not accuse you unless he had absolute proof,'
Teresa declared. 'He's not at all like that. He is very fair.
He will sift all the evidence and he will find the ruby in the
end. Then we will know who the thief really is and he will
punish them. You know, of course, that the ruby really
belongs to me.'

Catherine looked up at her.

'It was my mother's, so Lucía had no right to wear it!'

An awful suspicion dawned in Catherine's mind.

'You would never have stolen it,' she said.

Teresa's laugh was scornful.

'I could have taken it long ago if I had wanted to,' she
declared. 'Lucía is not so careful as she thinks. Anyone
could have gone into her bedroom and taken her jewel-
case, which she does not always bother to lock, but you
see, Lucía believes that they would not dare. Personally, I
think Manuel took it, although why I cannot tell you.'

'To get back at Lucía? She prized the ruby very much.'

'Only because it was something she had always coveted,'
Teresa flashed. 'It was Soria, as far as she was concerned.
But you may be right about Manuel. He might have wanted
to punish her by taking the thing she loved most of all. Do
you remember how she used to touch the ruby, holding it
close to her throat? It was the one thing she was sure
about and she was obsessed by it.'

'Which means that she must be terribly distressed by its
loss,' Catherine said quietly.

'We all are,' Teresa decided. 'Jaime, too, will be upset.
It was something of a family heirloom.'

To be brought back into the family when he finally married Lucía? Catherine pushed the hair back from her fore-head, feeling very tired.

'The storm is almost over,' she said, parting the curtains to look out. 'The thunder is rolling away.'

Rain was still falling in a steady downpour, but the night sky above El Teide was full of stars, making the whole world beneath them bright.

'All these stars,' said Teresa. 'They must be a good omen. We will find the ruby in the morning!'

CHAPTER SIX

LucÍa did not come down to breakfast. She had decided to stay in her room and allow them to search the garden un-hindered for the gem she declared they would no find.

Catherine, who had slept very little after the storm had subsided and Teresa had gone to her own room, came downstairs to find Ramón seated at the table in the *patio* with his feet up on an adjacent chair.

'I've been up since dawn,' he complained to justify the enormous breakfast he had obviously consumed. 'We've searched everywhere for that confounded ruby. Do you know what I think?'

'No.' Catherine sat down at the table beside him.

'I think Lucía lost it somewhere during the *fiesta*. If so, it will probably be found by some honest *peón* who will not know the real value and he will hand it to the police.'

'But Lucía was quite sure she had it when she got home from Orotava,' Catherine protested. 'Surely she couldn't be mistaken.'

'She might be trying to cover up for her own misfortune. Losing a valuable family heirloom is far more serious than misplacing a cheap trinket, don't you think?'

'She took such care of it. There was a little safety-chain to pin it to her dress.' Catherine poured herself a cup of coffee from the half-empty pot. 'It couldn't possibly have fallen while she was dancing.'

Ramón got to his feet.

'No, I suppose not, come to think of it,' he said slowly. 'It does look as if it was deliberately taken.'

'Ramón.' She looked across the table at him. 'Do you think I stole the ruby?' she asked.

'Goodness, no!' he exclaimed emphatically. 'I'm sure you

didn't. So is Jaime, although we haven't really discussed it.'

'Then—how do you know what he feels about me being seriously involved?'

'How do I know?' he repeated, coming to stand beside her. 'It's something I can't explain, but you can call it instinct, if you like. Jaime is a very fair person. He would not accuse you until he was absolutely sure, so you have nothing to worry about. Nothing at all.' He put a kindly hand on her shoulder. 'Cheer up, *querida*! It will not be long before we know the truth.'

'Have the police been called in?' Catherine asked nervously.

'Not yet.' Ramón went out into the sunshine. 'That will be a last resort, because Jaime has never been known to involve the family name in a scandal of any sort. He is very proud in that respect. Of course, if the ruby has been stolen he will go all the way in order to recover it.'

Catherine cut into an avocado pear. She had no appetite for her breakfast while the black cloud of Lucía's passionate accusation still hung over her. Although Teresa and now Ramón had assured her of their trust in her, there was still Jaime and, of course, Lucía herself.

'Is there anywhere else we could search?' she asked without much hope.

'Not around here,' said Ramón, 'but Jaime is trying to find Manuel. He has disappeared again, although Eugénie says he was here last night to sleep in his own quarters above the stables. Evidently he did not stay there very long, because he had gone when she went to call him this morning.'

Catherine could only think of Manuel with pity, for, if he had taken the ruby, Jaime would punish him.

'Do you think he has gone for good?' she asked.

Ramón shrugged.

'We cannot be sure. He has never known anywhere else but Soria. He was born here; he has always worked for us and Jaime takes his loyalty for granted. Manuel was a happy person till Lucía came on the scene,' he mused, 'but when he fell in love with her he became her slave. No doubt one day he will see how foolish he is.' He looked down at his mud-encrusted boots. 'Ah, well, back to the search! Jaime phoned Alex Bonnington, by the way, just to make sure that Lucía hadn't lost the ruby while she was there, but he got no reply. Perhaps you would try again, later on?'

Catherine nodded abstractedly, wondering what Alex would say when she heard of Lucía's irreplaceable loss.

She hadn't to wait very long for an answer. When she telephoned the bungalow there was still no reply and because Soria now seemed to be full of conflict she walked up through the garden to think more clearly.

Even here in the bright sunlight with the scent of frangipani heavy in the air and the flamboyant spears of a flame tree thrusting against the background green to make a brilliant splash of colour above her head, she could not think beyond Lucía's ugly accusation of the day before. She had meant every word she had said.

Coming eventually to the heavy oak door in the outer wall, Catherine hesitated. It was no use searching for the ruby beyond the door, but suddenly it seemed the only way to comparative peace of mind. Pulling it open, she found herself looking through the windscreen of Alex Bonnington's little white two-seater.

'Oh, Alex, you've no idea how glad I am to see you!' she exclaimed.

Alex took one look at her distressed face and the smile faded from her own.

'What's the matter?' she asked. 'Is it Lucía?'

'In a kind of way.'

Alex opened the car door.

'Get in!' she commanded.

When Catherine was settled in the seat beside her she reversed the car on to the main road.

'We'll drive a little way,' she suggested. 'You can tell me all about it.'

Catherine drew a deep breath.

'Why did you come?' she asked.

'I'd like to say it was because I am psychic and felt you needed me,' Alex answered, 'but it was really to return this.' She stretched into the glove compartment to produce a hastily-wrapped bundle from which the ends of the *mantilla* protruded. 'I knew you would be anxious about it.'

'Alex, how kind of you to bring it!' Catherine exclaimed. 'I didn't miss it until we got back and I phoned you, but you were out, and then there was so much else to think about.'

'Such as?'

'Lucía has lost her ruby.'

Alex pulled the car up at the side of the road.

'Lost it? But that's virtually impossible. She has a safety-pin on it strong enough to anchor a warship!'

A faint smile touched Catherine's lips.

'She believes it was stolen.'

'And she's accusing you?' It was amazing how quickly Alex had stumbled on the truth. 'But that's preposterous! What would you do with a ruby that size? It would be red-hot. Almost everybody this side of La Laguna knows it belongs to the Madrozas, including the police. Has Jaime called them in?'

Catherine shook her head.

'Not yet. I suppose he's giving—the thief time to repent and return it without creating a public scandal.'

Alex's lips closed in a tight line.

'Jaime is too particular in that respect,' she said. 'He could have cleared up those ugly rumours about Eduardo's death, but he wouldn't try to vindicate himself to the world at large because they'd judged him out of hand. The rumours were nothing, really—a flash in the pan—but the truth would have involved Ramón and so he chose to keep silent. Ramón, you see, could never accept Eduardo's authority after their father died. They quarrelled frequently and it was after one of those furious rows that Eduardo rode to his death. Jaime found him in one of the *barrancos* underneath his horse with a broken girth to account for the fall. He explained everything to the police quite satisfactorily, of course, but you know what rumours are.'

'Why are you telling me this, Alex?' Catherine asked, bewildered but hardly surprised by all she had just heard.

'Because I think you ought to know in case you might be judging Jaime too harshly. He is not the ogre you imagine him to be.'

Catherine made a small movement of protest.

'I always thought he would be fair,' she said faintly, 'but how can he believe in me when Lucía is so emphatic about my guilt?'

'Why must you think he would take Lucía's word against everyone else's?'

'Because he's going to marry her.'

Alex sat for a moment without answering.

'Lucía told you that, of course.'

'Yes, she said they would shortly announce their engagement.'

'And you believed her?'

'Certainly. What else could I do?'

'Distrust her completely,' Alex advised without a moment's hesitation. 'I don't think she has the faintest reason for believing that Jaime will marry her in the end. Up till a few weeks ago I would have said he was blissfully content with his bachelor existence, but now I'm not so sure. He's changed a great deal since he came back from Madrid,' she added. 'Perhaps the Marquesa has been talking some sense into his head. She was never very fond of Isabel at the best of times.'

'Isabel?' Catherine asked.

'Of course, you wouldn't know about their unfortunate love affair,' said Alex. 'It was a family thing, in the old Spanish tradition. The Madrozas and the Chamorros were very old friends and near enough neighbours to ensure that their children were seldom apart. Jaime and Isabel grew up together, accepting the fact that they would marry one day, and they were both happy enough with the situation. Then, two weeks before their engagement was to be an-

nounced publicly, Isabel met Raimundo de Triana, a penni-
less artist who came out to the Colony to paint. It was
love at first sight, as they say, but you can imagine how
everyone talked, and the endless sympathy Jaime had to
endure because there could be no doubt by that time that
he was deeply in love with his childhood playmate. People
called Isabel false and immature, but he would have none
of it, and when she went off to South America with de
Triana he wished her well. After that, there was nothing
for him but Soria. He worked with Eduardo day and night
to pay off their debts, and when Eduardo married Lucía he
moved up to Las Rosas so that he wouldn't be in their
way.'

Alex's explanation fell into a deep silence.

'I see now why he didn't want me at Soria,' Catherine
said presently. 'Any young woman would be an unhappy
reminder of his former love.'

'I think it was more than that,' said Alex. 'He imagined
that Teresa needed a firmer hand, the considered advice of
an older woman, perhaps. Once or twice I've tried to fill
the bill,' she added ruefully, 'but Teresa wouldn't listen. She
was determined to be a rebel, and that had been disastrous
at Soria before. Jaime was either too hard with her or altogether too lenient. He tried to take her father's place, but
Teresa would have none of it. And then there was Lucía.
She's brought him nothing but trouble since Eduardo died.
First of all, she demanded back all the money she had put
into the estate when Eduardo married her, and then she
offered it to Jaime with a condition attached.'

Catherine waited, not knowing what to say.

'In return for the money she was to make her home at
Soria for the remainder of her life. If Jaime married someone else it was to make no difference, but she expected to
marry him, in the end. That would consolidate her position
at the *hacienda* more than anything else, of course, but
either way she felt it would make little difference. Jaime
had given her his promise and she was family, anyway. He
would honour his commitments.'

Catherined turned her head away.

'He may not want to be rid of his responsibilities,' she said. 'This may be the sort of life he wants.'

'Do you honestly think so, Cathy?'

'I don't know what to think! Alex, sometimes I wish I'd never come to Soria in the first place, and yet——'

'It's no use regretting what is already done,' Alex declared practically. 'You're here, and you'll have to see this affair through to a reasonable conclusion. What do you imagine Lucía would say if you ran away?'

'I don't care about Lucía! It's what Jaime thinks that matters to me.'

Alex glanced at her with renewed interest.

'You know,' she said, 'that's exactly what I imagined.'

They had come back to the door in the wall and Catherine got out to open it.

'You'll come in, of course,' she said, holding it wide. 'You were on your way when we met.'

'Only to deliver your shawl. Do you know it belonged to Jaime's mother?'

'Teresa told me. It was terribly careless of me to leave it behind,' Catherine acknowledged.

'The fact that you wore it at all would incense Lucía,' Alex observed, driving through the gateway. 'It would be like the proverbial red rag to a bull, if you'll excuse my misuse of a gender or two!'

They drove the remaining distance to the house in silence, busy with their respective thoughts.

'I won't stay,' Alex decided when she saw the empty *patio*. 'Unless you think I can help?'

'Until we find the ruby I don't think anyone can,' Catherine said, 'but please stay for some coffee, at least. Jaime would expect it.'

For the first time they became aware of a figure hovering in the shadows and Lucía came out to the *patio* to join them. She was dressed in black once more, but the elaborate suit with its fine silk shirt deeply open at the neck to reveal a considerable amount of cleavage could hardly have been called widow's weeds.

'We do not see each other for months, Alex,' she observed, 'and then we meet twice in two days. Can I offer you a glass of wine since Jaime is not yet home? Or perhaps you would stay and share *merienda* with us? Ramón will be in quite soon,' she added pointedly.

Alex hesitated.

'Why not?' she agreed after a moment's consideration. 'I have no reason to rush back to Orotava except to feed the cat!'

Lucía had managed to ignore Catherine completely, even though she had allowed her hostile glance to rest for a moment on the *mantilla* in her hands. Catherine had unwrapped it to smooth out the creases before returning it to Teresa, but now she saw it as the final burning issue between them.

'I left it behind at the bungalow,' she explained, 'and Alex was kind enough to return it.'

Lucía looked as if she had only just become aware of her.

'Perhaps you will ask Teresa to come down,' she suggested with a thin smile. 'She has been searching my room. For the ruby,' she turned to explain to their unexpected guest. 'It has disappeared, so you can imagine how distressed I feel. You see, I am quite sure that it has been stolen.'

Catherine made her escape as quickly as she could, but she did not go immediately in search of Teresa. Instead, she turned along the colonnaded end of the *patio* and out into the garden where the shadows were gathering. A little wind had sprung up, stirring the fronds of the palms and scattering the petals from a nearby flame tree. They fell like confetti to the ground, lying in little scarlet pools on the cobbled path, and suddenly she shivered. Too many things were reminding her of the ruby. Even the poinsettias had the same rich colouring and the bougainvillea hanging down from the roof was the same vivid red. She had come to the garden to escape, but there was really no escape from Lucía's hatred.

It seemed a strong word to use, but what else could she call it, knowing herself innocent? Almost from the first moment of their meeting Lucía had resented her, but why? Why?

She walked urgently between the stone columns and out along the path, drawing the *mantilla* over her shoulders in a nervous little gesture of self-protection. If I could only do something, she thought. If I could only prove to Lucía how wrong she was.

The scent of the stephanotis was almost unbearably sweet and she turned away from it instinctively, remembering how she had smelt its heady fragrance when she had come to the *hacienda* for the first time. It would always remind her of Soria wherever she might go in the future, for it seemed only a matter of time now before Lucía would have her sent away.

A horse whinnied somewhere beyond the terracing and she watched as the rider came towards to house. Don Jaime de Berceo Madroza was returning home.

It seemed such a natural thing for her to be waiting there at the end of the garden to meet him, but she would never stand there in her own right. Lucía would see to that, and suddenly she knew why Lucía hated her so much. The older girl saw her as a rival for Jaime's affections, however ridiculous that might be.

He came on steadily down the path, a tall, straight figure on a pale horse, his head held proudly as he approached his home, and Catherine drew back into the shadows because her eyes were suddenly full of tears.

Jaime dismounted before the archway leading to the stables, turning as if he had sensed her presence under the colonnade.

'Cathy,' he said, 'is that you?'

'Yes.'

She brushed against the floss-silk tree as she moved towards him, and a scatter of pale pink blossom fell at her feet. Jaime did not move. He stood looking down at her as if he were seeing her for the first time, with the wedding *mantilla* on her shoulders and the scatter of petals falling all about her, and for one blinding moment she thought that he was about to kiss her again. She could almost feel the touch of his lips on her mouth, but instead he put his hands gently on her shoulders, turning her to face the light.

'Don't take this too much to heart,' he said. 'Lucía did not mean to be unkind. Sometimes I think she is obsessed with material things, and the ruby meant a great deal to her. All the same, I will not permit her to repeat her accusations.' His mouth hardened as he continued to look down into her distressed eyes. 'She is not always discreet in the things she says, but soon we will clear up the mystery of the ruby. Ramón has gone in search of Manuel, although he has not yet found him. If he is the culprit he will be punished.'

A deep feeling of revulsion stirred in Catherine's heart.

'Poor Manuel,' she found herself saying. 'What will happen to him?'

Jaime stiffened.

'If he is guilty he will not complain when he is justly punished.'

'You'll hand him over to the police?'

'Not if we recover the ruby.'

'I—suppose that's fair enough.'

She knew that he would have his own way of dealing with the situation. It would be swift and effective, and it would break Manuel's heart. He would be dismissed for ever from the place he loved, from the *hacienda* where he had been born and worked for most of his life, and he would never be able to come back. He loved Soria and the Madrozas, who had been his family ever since he could remember.

Slowly Jaime let his hands fall from her shoulders.

'You do not believe in a just retribution?' he asked almost coldly. 'But what other means have I to administer the estate? I depend on loyalty and honesty more than anything else. When my employees are dishonest they des-

troy themselves, and me. I have never met with it before in
a servant.'

But once, long ago, the girl you loved proved disloyal,
Catherine thought, and you have never been able to forget.
Never in all these years! Slowly she slipped the *mantilla*
from her shoulders.

'I must take this up to Teresa. I left it at Orotava and
Alex brought it back,' she explained, remembering how the
soft folds of the wedding *mantilla* had brushed against his
cheek as they danced and how he had kissed her afterwards, a kiss she would remember for ever, one kiss which
he had given lightly and had now forgotten. 'What is *fiesta*
without a kiss!' he had said as he set her free.

Shaken by the memory, she watched as he ran the folds of
the *mantilla* through his fingers.

'It is Madroza history,' he said thoughtfully. 'All the
Madroza brides have worn it for three generations, except
Lucía. I believe she was married in Madrid in a fashionable
hat.' He passed the *mantilla* back to her as they reached
the house. 'I suppose it does belong to Teresa.'

Lucía and Alex were still talking in the *salón* and he went
in to greet their unexpected guest while Catherine went
slowly up the staircase in search of her pupil. Teresa would
be glad to know that the *mantilla* was safely back at Soria.

She paused at the head of the stairs, wondering if Teresa
had finished her self-appointed task of searching all the
rooms for the missing jewel, but there was no sound anywhere on the upper floor. Teresa had either abandoned her
search or had searched to no avail.

At the door of her own room she paused again, deciding
to return the *mantilla* before she changed, but when she
looked into Teresa's room it was empty.

Carefully she spread the *mantilla* out on the bed, touching it gently for the last time before she turned away. One
day another bride would wear it, possibly Teresa herself.

The door of her own room was not quite closed, blown
open by the wind straying in through the long casement
from the garden, and her hand was on the knob when she

heard the first sobbing breath. Pushing the the door wide, she went in to find Teresa lying full length on her bed, her face buried in the lace coverlet, her hand clenched on the fine lawn handkerchief she had used to stem the first flood of her tears.

'Teresa, what's happened?' Catherine crossed swiftly to the bed. 'Why are you crying? Can you tell me and can I do anything to help?'

There was no immediate response. Teresa stiffened where she lay, but she did not turn to look at her.

'You can't do anything,' she muttered into the counterpane. 'You can't! Not now.'

'Teresa!' Catherine attempted to put her hands on her shoulders, easing her round. 'Please look at me and tell me what you are trying to say.'

As if she were dragging herself from some deep pit of despair, Teresa sat up and turned towards her. Her face looked strangely distorted, her eyes swollen with tears.

'Is it about the ruby?' Catherine asked, her heart thumping in her breast.

For a moment it seemed as if Teresa could not answer her. Her lips moved as if she might speak, but no words came, and then she looked quickly across the room, pointing with a trembling hand to the dressing-chest against the wall.

It was suddenly so still that they could hear the sound of voices from the *salón* below, and Catherine moved away from the bed. The second drawer of the dressing-chest had been pulled open. It was where she kept her underwear and for a moment she wondered why the fact should distress Teresa so much. And then, instinctively, she knew.

A whole lifetime seemed to pass as she crossed the polished floor, and then she was looking down into the open drawer at the ruby, lying like a spot of blood on the white garments she had folded away so carefully only a few days ago. It glittered like an evil eye, something so malevolent that she could not even touch it.

Teresa was still sitting on the bed, waiting, but Catherine could not bring herself to speak. A host of warring emotions were struggling in her heart—horror and pain and anguish, coupled with anger and, finally, despair. Who-ever had hidden the ruby in her drawer was determined that she should be accused of theft with ample evidence to sup-port the charge.

For a moment she could not believe that anyone at Soria would do such a thing, even Lucía, who disliked her so much, but the evidence of treachery was there before her eyes in the shape of the blood-red ruby lying in the drawer.

Slowly she turned to the crumpled figure on the bed, try-ing to clear her mind of everything but the simple facts.

'Teresa, when did you find this?' she asked in a voice which she hardly recognised as her own.

'Half an hour ago. I had searched all the other rooms, you see.' The misery in Teresa's eyes deepened. 'Say you didn't do it,' she begged. 'I couldn't bear it if you were sent away! You have made me happy here in so short a time. I could never face Soria as it was before you came.'

Catherine went to sit on the bed beside her.

'You have every right to think me guilty,' she said. 'Do you?'

Teresa raised distressed eyes to hers.

'No,' she said. 'I can't believe you would do such a thing. I think someone put it there to trap you so that Jaime would send you away at once. He would not be lenient if he thought you were a thief.'

'I realise that.'

Catherine was remembering the words Jaime had used in the garden less than an hour ago. 'I depend on loyalty and honesty more than anything else. When my employees are dishonest they destroy themselves, and me.' He would be harsh in his judgment once that dishonesty was proved beyond a shadow of a doubt, and here in her bedroom lay the irrefutable proof. She could not look at the ruby again, lying there like a stain on the white garments, nor for a moment could she think what to do.

'We must accuse Lucía,' Teresa said coldly. 'Of course it is her doing. She does not like you because she is jealous of you, just as she hated me from the beginning when she married my father. She did not want to have a daughter of my age, even a stepdaughter. You must realise how vain Lucía is. She knows that she is not beautiful and she wishes to dominate in other ways. Being indispensable to Jaime at Soria is one of them. If you had not been so young and pretty you could have stayed here for ever, for all Lucía cared.'

The unbridled hatred in the young voice was suddenly frightening.

'Teresa,' Catherine said slowly, 'had you any hand in this? Did you perhaps find the ruby elsewhere?'

Teresa jumped to her feet.

'How could I do such a thing?' she exclaimed. 'I would not involve you to get my own back on Lucía, even if we could prove she did it. I love you, Cathy! I've always wanted someone like you to—to talk to and confide in. Yes, I hate Lucía, but it is because she made me despise her, always taking away the things that belonged to my mother and destroying them or shutting them in a cupboard out of sight. I *wanted* to love her at first, but it became impossible. It was Lucía who had me sent away to the convent so that she might have complete power here at the *hacienda*.' She pressed the sodden handkerchief to her eyes. 'When my father died she even tried to keep me away from his funeral. She told me I could pray better for his soul at the convent. But Jaime would not have it. He had become master at Soria and so I came home, as I wanted to do. But now it will all be changed. You will be sent away and I will be alone again.'

'Alex is downstairs,' Catherine said automatically. 'She came to return your *mantilla*, which I'd left at the bungalow. I've put it on your bed.'

She seemed to be speaking in a dream where nothing was real and she was moving like an automaton. Teresa's theory that Lucía had deliberately placed the ruby in the drawer, or had it put there by someone else, could be no more than conjecture, and how to prove it if she had was quite another matter. Of course, Lucía would refute the suggestion, pouring scorn on it in the cold, deliberate way she had, and Jaime would believe her.

Why not? She was his sister-in-law, a member of his family, and he had known her for a very long time. Far longer than he had known Catherine, yet to her it seemed a lifetime since she had stepped off the plane at Madrid and found him waiting there, the proud, detached Spaniard with the looks of a *conquistador* even in the conventional city suit he had worn.

She tried to thrust the memory away, but it would not go. It was all tangled up now with so many other memories and with the inevitable love which she could no longer deny.

A kind of desperation took hold of her as she looked back at Teresa.

'What am I going to do?' she cried. 'I can't let this happen to me!'

Teresa crossed to the dressing-chest to stare down at the ruby.

'I don't think I would ever want it after this,' she said, 'even though it did belong to my mother. Lucía has—tarnished it.'

She picked up the stone to lay it beneath the mirror where it winked back at them in glittering derision. Catherine put her hand out, suddenly able to touch it. Putting it into the pocket of her dress, she turned towards the door.

'What are you going to do?' Teresa asked excitedly.

'I'm going to take it to Don Jaime. I'm going to prove to—everyone that I'm not a thief.'

Brave words, she had to admit, her throat choked with tears, but how to establish her innocence was quite another matter.

'Come down when you're ready,' she said to Teresa, the calmness of desperation in her voice. 'You'll have to wash your face and tidy your hair. Lucía has invited Alex to *merienda*. They'll be half-way through by now.'

The thought of hot drinking chocolate and sticky pastries nauseated her, but she would go through with the polite social ritual as much for Alex's sake as for Jaime's. She could not create a scene in front of a visitor, or the servants for that matter. She would go to Jaime when Alex had left and he was finally alone in his study going through the mail she had sorted for him that morning. The work they had done together would be over, too, she thought painfully. Everything would be at an end.

Alex was rising to go when she reached the *salón*.

'Come and see me soon,' she said, searching Catherine's pale face. 'Very soon,' she added beneath her breath as Lucía preceded her to the door.

Teresa was coming slowly down the stairs.

'Where have you been?' her stepmother demanded.

Teresa raised sullen eyes to hers.

'Looking for the ruby,' she answered, fixing her with a hostile stare.

But that was all. She did not say that she had found the missing jewel and Lucía did not ask.

Jaime went with Alex to her car and his sister-in-law turned towards the staircase.

'You will have to ring for more chocolate,' she told them. 'It must be quite cold by now.'

'Do you want anything to drink?' Teresa asked, lifting the silver chocolate-jug with an unhappy look in her eyes. 'I'll ring for Sisa.'

'Please don't! I couldn't eat anything.' Catherine's fingers had fastened over the gem in her pocket and it seemed to scorch her. 'Order some for yourself.'

'I'm not thirsty.' Teresa paced restlessly about the room. 'I wish Ramón would come home. There will be more rain —Teide is covered in cloud again. Manuel should be seeing to the irrigation, but Ramón will do it for him.'

'Ramón has gone to look for Manuel,' Catherine explained.

Teresa's eyes sharpened.

'I do not think he will find him,' she said. 'Not if Lucía has sent him away. That would be the end as far as Manuel was concerned.'

Catherine heard the car door slam and the sound of the engine as Alex drove away, and in the ensuing silence she felt very much alone. 'Come and see me soon,' Alex had said, as if she already knew there was trouble in the air.

Jaime came slowly back along the terrace, entering the hall by the *patio* door, but he did not cross to the *salón* where they were waiting. Instead, he went straight to the study, closing the door firmly against intrusion.

Catherine hesitated only for a fraction of a second while the ruby seemed to burn its way through her flesh.

'Will you go now?' Teresa asked.

She nodded, crossing the polished floor with a deliberation she found difficult to sustain as she knocked on the study door.

'*Adelante!*'

She paused to draw breath before she turned the painted knob and went in.

Jaime was seated at his desk with the neat piles of letters set out before him, ready to begin an evening's work which would last till the dinner gong sounded at ten o'clock. He looked up in vague surprise at her approach.

'Ah, Cathy!' he said. 'Thank you for tidying up in here. It is twice as easy to get to grips with everything now.'

She stood looking at him, stunned by what she had to say, although she knew that it must be said quickly. Withdrawing her hand from her pocket, she placed the ruby on the desk between them.

'I didn't take it,' she said, 'but you're not going to believe me.'

He looked at the ruby as if he had never seen it before.

'I didn't take it,' she repeated, thinking how futile her protestation must sound.

He took a long time to answer.

'Do you know who did?' he asked carefully, at last, his tone coldly impersonal as he looked back into her distressed eyes.

Catherine hesitated.

'I don't know for certain.'

'But you suspect someone? Someone in my household, perhaps?'

'Oh, Jaime!' She felt all her defences crumbling before his proud concern for his family name. 'I'm not accusing anyone because I have no proof. I came to give you back the ruby and to tell you that I was innocent. I hoped you would believe me, but—now I see how impossible that is. Everything points to my guilt, you see. Teresa found the ruby in one of the drawers of my dressing-chest. I don't know how it got there—I didn't steal it—but the fact remains that it was discovered in my room. That's all you have to go on, isn't it?' she rushed on. 'The evidence of my guilt!'

'Not quite.' He rose slowly to his feet, coming round the edge of the desk to stand beside her and seeming to tower over her in his superior height. 'I do not intend to judge you until I have gone into this more carefully. Blame or proof, how can we consider them impartially when so much emotion is involved?'

The little pulse beating at his temple suggested that he might be keeping powerful emotions in check with considerable difficulty, and she could not blame him for being angry.

'When did Teresa find the ruby?' he asked.

'About an hour ago.'

'While you were out with Alex?'

She nodded.

'And you had no idea it was there, in your drawer?'

'None whatever. I give you my word.'

Did it really matter, she wondered, when all the evidence was stacked against her?

A small, thin smile touched his lips.

'I know how you must feel,' she said. 'This is a dreadful

thing to happen, but I must defend myself. If you thought
me a thief——'

'Yes?'

'I couldn't stay here. In any case, I must go away.'

'Not so fast,' he said. 'I will make the decisions. You
must stay at Soria till we discover the truth.'

'Surely now that you have the ruby it doesn't matter
very much, unless—unless you want to punish me for something I haven't done.'

He laughed abruptly.

'You have an odd way of putting things, Cathy,' he said.
'I will punish the offender, of course, but until we know
exactly who it is I wish you to remain here. There must be
no scandal now that the ruby is safely returned, and you
will help to prevent it by staying where you are and continuing to instruct Teresa.'

'But that will be impossible!' she cried. 'How could I
pretend that everything was the same? Teresa knows, although she still believes in me because we've become
friends, and soon Doña Lucía will find out when you return the ruby to her.'

He turned his back on her for a moment.

'I want you to make me a promise,' he said almost
harshly.

'Anything,' she agreed.

'I want the discovery of the ruby to remain secret for
an hour or so. I want time to think and perhaps to act.'

'What's the use?' she cried. 'Even if you wait for a day
or a week Lucía will still accuse me.'

His jaw hardened as he turned back to face her.

'That may be so,' he agreed, 'but I have to be sure. You
believe that Lucía has become your enemy, but you have
no proof of that, either. Listen to me, Cathy!' He pulled
her round to face him. 'Four years ago I took on the full
responsibility of Soria. That meant the *hacienda* and the
peóns who work on the plantations, the servants here in
the house, and my brother's wife, to say nothing of Teresa.
It wasn't a promise to Eduardo before he died or anything

dramatic like that. It was just the natural thing to do. A
Spanish family is one unit, whether they are rich or poor,
and they are sheltered by the head of that family. You have
to understand that before you can understand me. Just as
our wide Córdoban hat shields a man from the heat of the
sun, so I must shelter my family from misfortune while I
can.'

'I know all this,' she agreed in a shaken whisper, 'but you
didn't expect the ruby to be stolen. It was a family heirloom.'

'Indeed, but I think I can survive the loss of a precious
stone, however valuable it might be. The ruby is nothing.
The important issue is that I am responsible for Lucía, just
as responsible, in a way, as I am for Teresa. She is my
brother's widow and I owe her a home.'

'Yes, I understand.'

'I wonder if you do!' He swept a handful of papers
across the desk in an impatient gesture which reminded
her incongruously of Ramón. 'Soria is beginning to pay
for the first time in a decade, and it is very much thanks
to the money Lucía invested in the estate when she married
my brother.'

'I see.' Her spirits were at their lowest ebb. He would
defend Lucía because Soria owed her so much, turning a
blind eye to anything she might have done. 'You've explained everything.'

'I don't think so,' he said immediately, 'but the rest can
wait. Have I your promise to keep quiet about the ruby for
the moment?'

She nodded.

'If that's what you want me to do,' she agreed, 'and I
suppose you have yet to be convinced that I'm innocent.'

'I must take your word,' he said, crossing to open the
door for her. 'Since you have given it.'

'Do you wish me to speak to Teresa?' she asked, pausing
on the threshold to look back at him.

'No, I will do that.'

It was the most unsatisfactory situation Catherine had

ever known, but she could only acknowledge his authority and keep her own counsel about the ruby.

The *salón* was empty when she reached it and the rain which had been threatening all day was already falling in great, heavy drops on the terrace so that she could not find solace in the garden, yet she could not go back into the house where she might so easily come face to face with Lucía. If they met it would be like the collision of the angry storm-clouds above El Teide.

She stood listening to the rain, hearing it falling on the tiled roof and running along the gutters and watching as it filled the ornamental troughs in the garden until they overflowed. It was tropical rain such as she had never seen before, falling relentlessly out of a leaden sky, but no doubt it would be good for the thirsty soil when it rained so seldom in this sun-kissed land. Water had to be stored in vast basins set into the hillsides against the possibility of drought and she knew the Ramón and Jaime had been supervising the construction of a new one for some time now. It had kept them busy between harvesting the vast banana crop and packing the tomatoes to make way for a further yield.

Restlessly she paced to the far end of the colonnaded way where the rain fell like a grey curtain between her and the garden trees, saturating the ground beneath them until it became a sea of mud, the weight of water snapping the heavy flower-heads from the wet branches to scatter them like thrown confetti at her feet.

Somewhere beyond the garden a sudden roar of water descended the planted terraces, rushing relentlessly downwards until it was finally trapped in one of the vast concrete dams. It was a terrible sound, driving fear into her heart. Where was Ramón and why didn't he come home?

For half an hour she stood there wondering about the immediate future, wondering what Jaime would do about the ruby; wondering about Lucía and her terrible obsession with power, and wondering, too, about Teresa when the time came for her to leave Soria altogether. She had an-

other year to do at the convent before she went to Madrid,
and a year could seem like an eternity to someone of
Teresa's age. She had passed through it all herself not so
long ago, the restless desire to leave the realm of childhood
behind for ever and step boldly into the adult future which
beckoned so seductively. Thinking of her own schooldays,
she realised how happy they had been, but she could not
caution patience when she had stretched out her hand so
eagerly to the future herself. Even when she had taken this
job and had come to Tenerife it had been with the odd,
pathetic hope in her heart that she would find a home.

And now, in a matter of days, perhaps, she would be
alone again.

The rain poured down relentlessly, the sound of it oblit-
erating all other sound. Surely there was enough water
now to fill all the catchment areas for many weeks to
come? She looked out at the tormented garden, already
despoiled by the weight of water and the ferocity of the
sudden wind which bent the palms almost to the ground
and tore great fronds from their upper branches to hurl
them across the terracing in wild abandon. Broken lilies
hung on their stalks, still gleaming bravely above the
ornamental pool, and the little pink geraniums which grew
almost wild around them hung their bright heads in dismay.

'It's worse than I expected.' Jaime was standing at her
elbow, frowning into the night. 'Do you know if Ramón
has come in?'

'I don't think so.' She turned towards him. 'I've been
out here for nearly an hour. Are you afraid for the new
dam?'

'That, and some of the others. The new one would
have taken the weight of most of this water if it had been
completed, but now all the strain will be on an old reservoir up in the hills. We were patching it yesterday, but the
new cement won't hold.'

She could see how worried he was and his need for
Ramón's help.

'Surely he will not stay away for long,' she said.

'I will need him immediately if this goes on.'

'Could I do anything to help in the meantime?' she asked.

He hesitated.

'You could stand by the telephone till it goes out of order,' he said. 'It won't be long now, with all this wind and rain about, but I must be in contact with Orotava for as long as possible. The surrounding estates will all be affected if our dam breaks.'

'I'm sorry,' she found herself saying. 'You could have done without this.'

'It could mean life or death for Soria.' His voice was suddenly harsh above the sound of the falling rain. 'We need water, and then we get too much. It is always the way, but I should have been prepared for it.' He struggled into a heavy riding cape. 'Can I leave you in charge at this end till Ramón gets back?'

'I want to help,' she said.

He stood looking down at her, buttoning the cape close under his chin.

'*Gracias*, Cathy!' he said. 'Will you tell Ramón to join me as quickly as he can? I'll be at the west dam where most of the damage could occur.'

She watched him go, a tall figure stooping a little against the onslaught of the rain, his head bowed, his proud face no longer confident as he strode off into the night.

Lucía came from the direction of the kitchens.

'Who was that?' she demanded.

'Jaime. He has gone to look at the new dam. He's afraid it won't stand up to the rush of water if the rain continues.'

Lucía's expression changed as a look of triumph dawned in her eyes.

'He may have need of me again,' she said. 'My father's money saved Soria once before, but now Jaime has managed to pay it almost all back to me to save his pride. He has impoverished himself to recover his independence, but we shall see!'

'You can't be *glad* that this has happened,' Catherine gasped. 'That the rain may wash away the dam.'

'Glad, no, but I am a fatalist, Miss Royce,' Lucía declared. 'I believe that what will be cannot be averted. You will disagree with me, of course, but that is of no consequence. You are not a part of Soria, as I am. You will return to your own country quite soon and your time here will be forgotten.'

The logic of her statement could hardly be denied, but Catherine was determined to hold her own while she remained at Soria in the present emergency.

'Jaime has asked me to stand by the telephone,' she explained, 'and to contact Ramón as soon as he comes in.'

'Ramón could be anywhere,' Lucía declared. 'He looks after his own amusement, that one!'

'He has gone in search of Manuel.'

Catherine had meant to defend Ramón from Lucía's cynicism, but the effect of her words was electric.

'Manuel?' Lucía cried. 'What has he to do with Soria now? I have dismissed him. He was my own servant and I sent him away.' Any colour which might have been in her sallow cheeks had faded to a dull putty. 'Ramón had no right to go after him of his own accord.'

'I think Jaime knew he was searching for Manuel,' Catherine said coldly, 'and Manuel could be needed in the present emergency.'

'They will not find him,' Lucía declared emphatically. 'He has gone for good.'

For no very clear reason Catherine's heart sank.

'Ramón will come back, in that case,' she said with confidence. 'He is needed here.'

It was another hour before Ramón made his appearance, soaked to the skin after a long ride in the rain. Teresa and Catherine had made several telephone calls in the meantime to be quite certain that the neighbouring estates were still in contact and that they hadn't suffered any damage.

'Where's Jaime?' he demanded. 'I got here as quickly as I could when I saw the storm brewing.'

'He wants you at the west dam,' Catherine explained. 'He seemed to be worried about the water and the concrete not holding.'

'I thought he might be,' he said. 'I'll go right away.'

'Did you find Manuel?' Teresa asked.

He shook his head.

'I tried most of his old haunts along the coast without any luck.'

'Lucía sent him away.'

Ramón paused at the door to look at her.

'Did she, indeed?' he mused. 'How do you know?'

'She has just told Catherine, although she did not give any reason.'

'She will have a good enough reason of her own. Damn the rain!' Ramón exploded. 'We'd made a good job of that reservoir.'

There had been pride in his voice, pride in a task well done, and for the first time Catherine realised that she could take him seriously.

'We're hanging on here in case we have to phone for help or give the others a warning,' Teresa explained. 'The Serranos will be most affected if the dam goes. Pablo is going up to help Jaime, and Victoria will stand by their phone. If you have to stay out all night we will bring up refreshments,' she added. 'Catherine can drive the car.'

'I wouldn't say "no" to something hot later on,' Ramón agreed, pocketing a handful of the little sweet cakes which still remained on the table as he passed. 'I haven't eaten since this morning.'

'What, no *tapas*!' Teresa exclaimed. 'You must be wasting away without your crayfish and sausages!'

'I will do greater justice to your picnic basket when you bring it!' he laughed, going off to collect a fresh horse.

CHAPTER SEVEN

It was midnight before the dam broke. After dinner Teresa and Catherine had packed a large basket with the food which would carry best, *lomo embushado*, and mountain ham and some choice pieces of boiled beef and chicken, together with salad and cheese and several bottles of home-made wine to augment the two large flasks of hot coffee *con leche* which Eugénie filled while they waited.

'We've got enough for an army here,' Catherine observed as Teresa added a large bowl of potted crab to their collection.

'We'll need it all because we will have a small army to feed,' Teresa assured her. 'Everyone who can possibly help will be there, the Serrano *peóns* as well as our own. We will brew more coffee when we get to the dam.'

Lucía came to inspect the hamper.

'I will come later on,' she said. 'It will be best if I stand by the telephone.'

They were still in contact with the outside world, which was amazing considering how much water must have seeped into the overhead conductors, but it seemed that Lucía had another reason for wanting to remain at Soria. Did she perhaps fear that Manuel might return to be questioned by Jaime?

Catherine had no time to think of Lucía now. All that concerned her was the thought of Jaime out there in the wild night fighting for the *hacienda*'s very life.

'It's a stiff drive,' Teresa warned when they were finally in the car, 'but there was nobody left to take us now that Manuel has gone. Pedro and Fernando will be at the dam or somewhere else on the terracing if the water has come down.'

There seemed to be nothing in the whole, dark world

beyond the boundary wall but water. It fell from the sky and rushed madly down every available slope, carrying sand and soil and rocks with it; it slid secretly beneath trees and gushed triumphantly over every man-made barrier in its way, carrying wooden bridges along with it as if they were toys; it flooded into little reservoirs and out again on the other side, spilling in a reckless waterfall to the terraces below, and now it seemed as if there was a stealthy quality about its progress which made it far more frightening to behold.

Catherine gripped the steering-wheel, concentrating only on the road ahead.

'How far?' she asked.

'About another mile.'

Already they had come two and the road had deteriorated all the way.

'If the dam goes we'll be cut off,' Teresa remarked.

'Don't be so cheerful!'

'I was only sounding a timely warning.' Teresa sat close up against the windscreen. 'Now I can't see a thing!' she complained.

'You're the navigator,' Catherine told her. 'We simply have to get through.'

The screenwipers were practically useless, sweeping to and fro to little effect, while the mud on the road seemed to be deepening with each turn of the wheels. Whole sections of what had been a sandy surface were now a veritable sea of mud, and when they did come to a rocky part the car tended to slip sideways into a skid.

'I wish I was more experienced,' Catherine gasped, righting it for the third time. 'I'm a city driver, I'm afraid.'

'We will soon be there,' Teresa encouraged her. 'I think I can see lights ahead. Si! Si! They are on the *carretas* and there are others in the *barranco*. I wonder what they are doing down there. Look! they are moving.'

'I can't look at the moment,' Catherine pointed out. 'It's as much as I can do to keep the car on the road.'

Teresa continued to peer anxiously through the wind-

screen, her face almost pressed against it, and at last
Catherine was able to make out the vague shapes of men
and machines spaced out along the road ahead of them.

'Stop here!' Teresa commanded. 'We must go in search
of Jaime.'

Catherine pulled the car to the side of the road and they
stepped out into the mud and rain to be met by a howling
wind which buffeted them unmercifully as they trudged
towards the nearest group of lights. Before they reached
it, however, a tall, recognisable figure strode quickly towards them.

'Cathy! Teresa!' Jaime took them both firmly by the
arm. 'You should not have come. There is still danger.'

'You need food,' Teresa said practically, 'and the car's
full of it, to say nothing of hot coffee and wine!'

'I saw your lights coming along the road.' He sounded
brusque, but it may have been his method of combating
an almost overwhelming tiredness. 'There are a great many
of us, but even one hot drink will be welcome. Pablo Serrano brought up a waggon a few minutes ago and Ramón
is sharing out the food in the *barranco*.'

'Why are you working down there?' Teresa wanted to
know.

'If the dam goes we hope to channel most of the water
into the *barranco*, away from the terraces,' he explained,
'but we are working against time. We have to dig a long
way, but with any luck we could make it.' The light of
challenge in his eyes cancelled out the grimness of his expression as he looked down at them. 'You must not wait,'
he decided. 'When we have unpacked the car you must return home.'

'We will stay,' said Teresa, the line of her jaw as determined as his. 'You could do with another pair of hands
—two pairs of hands!'

'No, Teresa,' he said. 'I wish you to return. It could be
dangerous when the water comes down.'

'*You* will be in danger,' she protested.

'That is different.'

'And Ramón.'

'That is also different.'

'Because you are men!' Teresa scoffed. 'But I am equally strong and Catherine would help if you would let her.'

He shook his head.

'You see that we have already enough help,' he said, indicating the line of men digging frantically in the feeble light of the hurricane lamps. 'There is nothing else to do except dig.'

'And make more coffee when this is finished,' Teresa insisted, turning back to the car. 'We have brought a stove.'

Jaime looked down at Catherine.

'Thank you for coming,' he said. 'If we can save the terraces I'll have won through.'

The desire to reach up and kiss him almost overcame her. He had taken off the waterproof cape to work more quickly and he was soaked through, his hands and face stained with the red mud of the terraces where he had toiled for the past six hours, shoulder to shoulder with the *peóns* in an effort to save his inheritance. It was an effort for Soria and the family he loved, for Ramón, and Teresa, and Lucía, who were all dependent on him.

'You will win,' she said, confident in the quality of the man. 'It would be too cruel otherwise.'

'Nature does not choose her victims,' he said laconically, 'but I can insist that you return to Soria before there is serious trouble here. If the dam breaks before the new channel is finished——'

He shrugged, aware that he had no need to spell out the details to her as she stood beside him in the angry night.

Catherine followed him to the car where Teresa was already unpacking the hamper.

'How will we do it?' she asked. 'Will we go down to the men?'

He shook his head.

'I will send Manuel to you.'

'Manuel?' Teresa looked up at him in amazement. 'When did he come?'

'Around eight o'clock, when we most needed him.' There was pride and satisfaction in his voice. 'He knew we would be in trouble when he saw the storm gathering over Teide.'

'Well, I'm blessed!' exclaimed Teresa because she could think of nothing else to say.

'We needed him because he had done most of the work on the dam with me,' Jaime went on to explain. 'In spite of going off without permission, Manuel has the welfare of Soria deeply at heart and he's worked like a Trojan these past few hours. I have never seen anyone quite so wet!' His mouth twisted in a wry smile. 'I cannot see myself, of course!'

He strode off down the hill, swinging the lantern he had picked up to guide him in the darkness.

'Manuel,' said Teresa, 'just couldn't stay away. He loves Soria, you see, almost as much as Jaime does.'

'And you!'

There was a long silence while Teresa considered the point.

'Cathy, I don't know,' she said at last. 'When it's like this I love Soria with all my heart. Like Jaime, I would give my life for it, but when things are going well, when one day follows another with so little to do, I'm not sure. I think that I must go out into the world to dance, perhaps, because it is the way I can express myself best.' She sighed. 'But meanwhile I will go back to the convent, I suppose, and then to the University in Madrid to learn to be something-or-other, which will suit my family!'

'A few years,' said Catherine. 'They're very little in a lifetime. I know that sounds like the advice of an old fuddy-duddy, but you'll see how true it is—afterwards. And now,' she added lightly, 'back to the present! Have we enough mugs to go round, do you think?'

'Most of the *peóns* will have their own,' Teresa said,

hacking at the strips of pork. 'I wish Jaime had waited for something to eat.'

'He may come back,' Catherine suggested, 'before we go.'

'Go?' Teresa turned with the carving knife in her hand, looking incredibly fierce in the uncertain light. 'You can go, Cathy, but I'm staying. I don't care what Jaime says!'

'Don't let's argue about it. We can make a second run with more food early in the morning,' Catherine suggested, feeling that diplomacy was the better part of valour with Teresa in her present mood. To tell her that Jaime had ordered them to return to Soria for their own safety would only complicate matters.

Teresa peered into the beam of the car headlights which they had left on.

'For heaven's sake, what's this?' she cried.

A small, squat figure leading a donkey was coming towards them, water dripping from his *poncho* and streaming from the brim of the wide *sombrero* he wore close down over his eyes.

'It's Manuel,' Catherine said quietly. 'Don't laugh!'

'No, he will take it as an insult,' Teresa agreed, 'but just look at him!'

Manuel came round to the back of the car where they were sorting out the food, bowing on sight of them, and a small river of rain cascaded from the scooped brim of his hat to fall into the mud at his feet. Manuel and water were synonymous at that moment. It even dripped from his hands as he held them out for the flasks, and came out of the tops of his boots.

'Ah, Manuel!' Teresa said, 'you have returned to help us. I'm sure Don Jaime could not have done without your assistance.'

Lucía's former servant beamed his appreciation, wiping away the little stream of water that dripped from the end of his nose.

'I thank you, *señorita*,' he said, not quite looking at her. 'I could not see the *hacienda* in trouble without coming to your assistance. Don Jaime already understands.'

'We are grateful, Manuel,' Teresa assured him, straight-faced. 'Already you have done much good work by digging a way into the *barranco*.'

'It is not yet finished.' Manuel turned away with the flasks and a basket of mugs over his arm. 'We work like crazy now to beat the water.'

When he raised his head to look at her the water poured from the brim of the now sagging *sombrero* down his back, but he did not seem to notice it. What he had lost in comfort he had gained in stature from Teresa's praise.

They brewed tea and coffee on the picnic stove in the boot of the car, sheltered by Teresa's riding-mac as an awning, although gusts of wind-lashed rain found them from time to time, almost extinguishing their source of heat.

Ramón came up with the empty flasks to have them refilled.

'The coffee went like a bomb,' he declared, dripping all over them. 'If this doesn't work I'll never put another spade in the soil for the rest of my life!'

In spite of his discomfort, he was really enjoying himself, using his initiative in the *barranco* while Jaime gave his undivided attention to the dam.

'We may just do it,' he said. 'Jaime thinks we have got about an hour.'

'Will it never go off?' Teresa looked up at the relentless heavens. 'El Teide is a monster I could never love again!'

'You will,' Ramón predicted, 'as soon as he smiles on us again. You are like a woman in love, Teresa, all anger and frustration when you see the dark side of your lover's face, but ready to embrace him as soon as he relents.'

'What nonsense you talk!' Teresa scowled at him. 'I see that Manuel has returned,' she observed. 'Where did you find him?'

'I didn't. He came back of his own accord. He could see that he was needed at Soria in an emergency.'

'Aren't we all?' said Teresa. 'You had better get back to

the *barranco* when we have filled your flasks.'

'I'll take one down to Jaime, or perhaps you could get as far as the dam?' he suggested as an afterthought. 'It isn't very difficult.'

'I'll go,' Catherine offered. 'I'll take a lantern.'

Once she was away from the car her eyes adjusted to the darkness and she could see the path to the dam studded with lights from other hurricane lamps. It seemed, too, that the sky above El Teide had lightened a little, although the rain was still falling. There was no clear road along the terracing, only the one narrow path which had been carved out by the dam-builders while they worked. Picking her way carefully, she made out the vague outline of the little reservoir and the figures of the men still at work on it. Jaime was there, carrying sandbags with the rest, piling stones and shouting instructions as he went along. It was almost midnight and the dam still held.

He saw her when she reached the end of the path and came angrily towards her.

'Go back!' he commanded. 'This is no place for you, Cathy, however much you want to help.'

'I brought you some coffee.' She held out the flask. 'Please drink it. You can't go on being cold and wet for ever.'

Their fingers touched as he took the flask.

'Have you had anything to drink yourself?' he asked roughly.

'I'll get something when I go back to the car. Ramón was up there a moment ago and he took another flask back to the *barranco*.'

'I couldn't have managed this on my own,' he admitted. 'I didn't think Ramón could work so well and I hope he realises that I appreciate the fact.' He poured some coffee into the top of the flask, holding it out to her. 'I insist that you drink this,' he said. 'You look like a forlorn ghost.'

'You're still worried about Soria,' she said, sipping the hot liquid. 'I wish the rain would stop.'

He glanced over her shoulder.

'So do I. We've done all we can up here. The wall will go, sooner or later, and everything now depends on Ramón at his end.'

'They're digging like mad. Manuel is down there with him. He came to the car for the food, but he would not eat up there. He wanted to get back to the *peóns*.'

He refilled the top of the flask when she had finished and drank deeply.

'That was good,' he said. 'You have put new life into me!' Then, more seriously: 'Cathy, I beg you to go back to the house and take Teresa with you. You are both in great danger.'

She could see that he did not want her to stay and there was really nothing they could do to help except to return with another hot meal in the morning.

'I'll have to persuade Teresa,' she said with a forced smile, 'but I think I can.'

'*Hasta mañana!*' he said, putting his hands gently on her shoulders to turn her back along the way she had come.

Until tomorrow! But she could be seeing him for the last time. He had admitted to great danger for Teresa and herself, so it would be equally dangerous for him and Ramón and Manuel and all the estate labourers who had toiled half the night to save Soria.

Standing on the high ground above the dam, she looked back for a fleeting glimpse of him, but there was nothing to be seen in the darkness but the glow-worm lights of the hurricane lamps strung out along the path.

'Did you find Jaime?' Teresa wanted to know.

'Yes, I found him.' Catherine got in behind the steering-wheel. 'He wants us to go home, Teresa, and—come back later with more food. Hot soup, perhaps. I saw Eugénie preparing it before we left.'

Teresa hesitated.

'It's no use pretending,' she said. 'The dam's not going to hold and everything will be swept away. It will be the end of Soria as we know it, and Jaime will be up to his ears in debt again. Which means he'll be completely in Lucía's power, because she will offer him the money, as she did before. He has paid most of it back to her; this next harvest would have been the end of all his obligations to my stepmother.'

Catherine gazed blankly through the windscreen.

'We won't talk about it,' she said unsteadily. 'He mustn't fail.'

'I think we are going to need a miracle, in that case,' said Teresa, getting in beside her.

'It may be wishful thinking,' Catherine said when she had started the engine, 'but it looks as if the rain is easing off a little.'

'It won't make any difference to the reservoir,' Teresa pointed out. 'The weight of water will still be there, pressing against the dam.'

Catherine drove even more carefully than she had done on the way up, taking each bend at no more than walking pace, but suddenly, on a sloped curve, the back wheels slid away and the car went into an uncontrollable skid. Nothing she could do would right it, and in a split second which seemed more like an eternity they were sliding into the wet scrub and down a bank into oblivion.

The car stopped with a sudden jerk, but all the lights had gone out and it was impossible to see what had broken their fall. On one side a group of stunted trees clung to the mountainside; on the other there was nothing.

'Teresa,' Catherine called in a shaken voice, 'where are you?'

'Out here!' The car was tilted at an angle and Teresa's head appeared at the open door. 'I was thrown out. How about you?'

'I'm all right,' Catherine hastened to assure her. 'We'll have a bruise or two in the morning, I expect, but that's nothing.' Her voice was not quite steady. 'Oh, why had this to happen? I lost control completely. There was absolutely nothing I could do.'

Teresa was peering into the darkness.

'At least it's stopped raining,' she said laconically.

'I wonder where we are.'

'Halfway down the mountain, by the look of things, and certainly not on the road. Do you often come this way?'

'Teresa, don't joke! I've damaged Jaime's car and got us into an awful predicament,' Catherine sighed. 'Do you think we can climb back on to the road?'

'Once we've got our bearings we'll have to try,' Teresa decided. 'Nobody will have the time to come in search of us. Watching the dam is far more important.'

For ten minutes they sat where they were to get their breath back.

'I wonder why disasters never happen singly,' Teresa mused. 'This wasn't on the cards at all. We were only trying to help. Don't worry too much about the car,' she added impulsively. 'Jaime will understand that it was an accident. He isn't really an ogre, you know.'

'I—never thought he was.' Catherine held her breath. 'I thought him overbearing and proud and arrogant at first, but that has all changed now.'

'Because you're in love with him?'

Catherine's eyes filled with tears.

'Yes.'

Teresa sat in silence, digesting her confession.

'That explains everything,' she said, sliding out of the car again. 'We'd better go.'

Catherine eased herself from behind the steering-wheel. In the darkness sounds came down to them clearly: the running of the water in the gullies; a distant roar of thunder beyond El Teide; the whine of the wind in the branches of the nearby trees, and then, suddenly, the sound of a man's voice above them on the road.

'Stay where you are!' it commanded. 'I'll go down on my own. You look after the horses.'

'Jaime!' Teresa yelled with all her might. 'We're here. Down here beside the trees.'

Stones rattled towards them as he clambered down the slope and presently they saw him scrambling towards them. It looked as if he had seen the car from some vantage-point above the trees, but he was not concerned about it. He grasped Catherine by the arms.

'Thank God you're safe!' he exclaimed. 'Are you hurt?' He turned towards Teresa.

'Not so much as your car,' she returned. 'We're shaken, of course, and Cathy has lost the power of speech!'

For a moment Catherine clung to Jaime's arms.

'I couldn't stop it,' she confessed. 'The wheels just slid away.'

'Don't worry about the car,' he said, breathing deeply. 'I knew something like this must have happened when I didn't see your headlights at the hairpin bend.'

'You left the dam?' Catherine said. 'Oh, Jaime, I'm sorry! This was such a little thing.'

'It could have cost you your life,' he returned harshly. 'With a lot of luck the dam might hold till I get back.'

'He took a chance to save us,' Teresa murmured. 'How like Jaime!'

They heard the dam give way as they reached the top of the bank. The awful slide of the water, an insidious, stealthy sound, seemed to fill the whole world as they stood there utterly incapable of doing anything about it, and Jaime turned his face towards El Teide as if cursing the mountain that had brought such disaster upon them. In the next moment, however, he was the man of action.

'Wait here, on the road,' he commanded. 'I'll send a waggon for you and then you can go back to Soria and bring more food. No matter what has happened at the reservoir we'll be here for the rest of the day.'

'What about Ramón—and Manuel?' Teresa asked.

'We must hope that they were ready for the water.' His face in the pale lantern-light was grim. 'Stay here,' he repeated. 'Don't try to follow me.'

The peón who had held his horse in readiness on the road helped him to mount, climbing on to the back of his own pony to lead the way.

'Remember,' Jaime called, 'go straight back to Soria. You can do nothing up here.'

They waited in the darkness for the estate waggon, reluctant to discuss what he might have found on his return to the dam.

'If anything terrible has happened to Ramón, Alex Bonnington will never forgive herself,' Teresa declared.

'Alex?'

'Oh, they were in love for a time and then Ramón broke it off. He told Alex he wanted to be free. "And free he shall be until he comes to his senses," Alex said. "For ever free if he likes!" Wasn't that typical of Alex? Then, when Ramón wanted her to go back to him she told him that he couldn't blow hot and cold with her.' Teresa sighed. 'She said he would have to have more to show for his life than a Don Juan image and a wish to be a reporter. Naturally, Ramón went off in a huff, but I think he has stuck it out at Soria just to prove to Alex that he could.'

'What about the reporting?' Catherine asked, her thoughts elsewhere.

'He could do that and help at Soria, too,' Teresa said. 'He's been writing up local events for years, but if he really wanted to make a full time career of it he could go to Madrid or Barcelona or somewhere like that.'

'Would Alex go with him?'

Teresa shrugged.

'I think she would, if he really wanted her to go.'

The waggon drew up beside them. It was one of the covered type used for transporting the packers from one station to another in the heat of the sun.

'Get in!' Teresa said. 'I'll sit up in front beside Manuel.'

Catherine hadn't recognised the driver, but now she saw that it was indeed Manuel, bereft of the ridiculously large *sombrero* and wearing a waterproof cape instead of the gaily-coloured *poncho*. He laid his whip across the horse's back and they plunged on down the road, taking the treacherous bends with ease. Experienced horses didn't slip in the mud, Catherine thought, like temperamental cars! No one used a car at the *hacienda* when a horse was more readily available, yet they would need the car for long distances and she had successfully wrecked it. Lucía would be the first to miss it for her periodic jaunts to the *puerto* or in to Santa Cruz.

It seemed an eternity since they had last seen Lucía, but she would be waiting for them at Soria. Catherine looked out through the gap in the tarpaulin where she could just see Manuel's back, and he seemed to have shrunk in size since their last encounter at the dam.

When they came to the house he halted the waggon just short of the *patio*, waiting for them to get out.

'Have something hot to drink before you return, Manuel,' Catherine suggested as Teresa made her way towards the kitchens.

He shook his head.

'I am needed up there. Much work is still to be done.'

'Well, at least take some soup back with you.'

'I will wait,' he agreed.

Catherine turned away.

'*Señorita!*' He came up behind her. 'You have much to forgive me for. I knew that the *señora* was going to accuse you, but I kept quiet because I did not know what to do.'

Catherine swung round in astonishment.

'Manuel, are you talking about Doña Lucía's ruby?'

He nodded.

'She did not want me here, although we had been lovers,' he said, his dark eyes suddenly lit with passion. 'But that is true no longer,' he declared. 'I have been a fool. I allow her to play with my affections and I care too much when she is suddenly cold. Now I care no longer. I will marry a *señorita* of my own station in life instead and live peacefully.' He raised his head disdainfully. 'She tried to buy me off with the ruby, but I returned it to her, and that is when she put it into your room. This I watched,' he declared. 'She is full of spite, that one, although once I loved her much.'

'Manuel!' Catherine gasped incredulously, although all the pieces seemed to be fitting together like a jigsaw. 'You're quite sure about this?'

'Why would I say it if it was not true?' he demanded,

grievously affronted that she should doubt his word.

'No, I'm sure you wouldn't.'

'I have told all this to Don Jaime,' Manuel went on, 'and he is very angry. He will punish Doña Lucía in his own way. She would like to marry him, but I don't think that could ever be.'

'What a mess we've made of everything!' Catherine exclaimed.

'This I agree,' he returned, flicking his whip against his muddy riding-boots. 'But Don Jaime will speak to you about it on his return.'

And meanwhile there was Lucía, Catherine thought, her heart pounding like a sledgehammer. It was difficult to believe that anyone could have proved so treacherous, but the evidence of the ruby lying in her drawer was too clear to refute. No one else but Lucía would have done such a thing, because Lucía had been fighting for her life. All she had ever wanted was to remain at Soria as mistress of the *hacienda* and she would have married Jaime without love to achieve her goal.

And Jaime? What did he really think of his sister-in-law now that he knew the truth? Even with the evidence of Manuel's statement, would he still marry Lucía to save Soria from ruin?

She could not believe that he would, and the very fact that he had left Soria to its fate up there in the mountains to rescue them seemed to underline her faith in him. Her safety and Teresa's had meant more to him even than the *hacienda*, which was his birthright.

Lamps were burning in the kitchens and Eugénie was ladling soup into two large containers while Teresa looked on. There was no sign of Lucía.

'She has gone to the mountains,' Eugénie said when they asked. 'Riding that mad black horse which is more like a devil than a natural animal! She will be too late if the dam is already down, and men do not trust a woman who is always poking her nose into what is their business!'

Catherine helped to carry the soup out to the covered waggon.

'Better keep our noses to ourselves!' Teresa said with a grin. 'Manuel, can you manage on your own?'

'Sí, señorita, I will manage very well.' Manuel cracked the long whip and rode away.

'Lie down for a while,' Teresa suggested, 'and Eugénie will waken us at five o'clock. Then it will be time to go back to the reservoir with some more soup. You look very tired. I'm dropping,' she added. 'I'll be asleep before my head touches the pillow!'

It was impossible for Catherine to sleep with so many conflicting thoughts racing round in her mind, and long before Eugénie came to call them she was up and dressed and waiting for Teresa.

A pale, thin dawn was breaking as they set out in the little cart which Teresa said she could drive. It was drawn by one of the sturdy cream ponies and seemed adequate for their journey, but the pace was almost unbearably slow.

'I wonder what we'll find when we get there,' Teresa mused, voicing Catherine's anxious thoughts. 'If anyone has been hurt they would have been brought down by now.'

It was a hope to hold on to as they made their second trek into the mountains, but this time the going was easier. In the rapidly strengthening light the sure-footed little pony covered the ground with confidence, and already the thirsty earth had absorbed much of the rain of the day before. The gullies were still full of water, and where there was a steeper slope it plunged down to the terracing in a miniature cascade, sending up little plumes of spray into the cool air, but the overall volume seemed to be less. El Teide sat above it all, serene and watchful, with only a single white cloud hovering about his head to suggest the havoc of the night before.

'He is a demon!' Teresa cried. '*Now* he can smile!'

They reached the spot where the car had left the road.

'They're bringing it up,' Catherine said in some surprise. 'It wasn't so very far down the hillside, after all.'

'It seemed as if we had gone right to the bottom,' Teresa mused, pulling up to look. 'They're using ropes. It must be some of the equipment from the dam.'

Catherine was looking round for Jaime, but he was nowhere to be seen. Obviously he had left the recovery of the car to someone else.

'We'd better press on,' said Teresa, flicking her whip above the pony's ears. 'I know how hungry Ramón can get, especially when he has been out on the mountains for half the night!'

Her anxiety was showing through the glib chatter by the time they had reached the dam.

'Look! Down there,' she pointed. 'The water is all running away into the *barranco*!' She pulled the cart up with a yell of delight. 'They made it!' she cried. 'Ramón must have dug out the last section of the channel just in time. Oh, Cathy, isn't it wonderful? A real miracle, because not one drop of that water has gone down into the valley!'

Catherine closed her eyes for a moment, hardly able to believe what they had seen.

'It's the answer to a lot of prayers,' Teresa rushed on. 'It could have meant absolute disaster, you know, taking years of hard work to put right. But now Soria is saved and Jaime won't have to work like a slave to build it all up again.'

He came up the narrow path towards them, weary and unshaven but triumphant.

'It's all over,' he said, gazing down at the swirling brown water as it plunged harmlessly into the *barranco*. 'Ramón has certainly excelled himself. He worked like someone possessed—for Soria.' He passed a hand over his mud-caked face. 'It's been quite a night,' he observed, looking up at them with the new sun glinting in his eyes. 'Thank you for all you have done.'

'Like wrecking your car,' Teresa suggested, able to smile at last. 'I don't suppose you'll ever forgive us for that.'

'It was nothing.' He dismissed the accident with a brief wave of his hand. 'There is very little damage—a scratch or two, no more—but for a moment I thought you were dead.' He looked from one of them to the other. 'It was a narrow escape,' he added.

Teresa jumped down from the cart and he turned to help Catherine.

'I'm sorry,' she apologised. 'It would seem I'm not a very good driver either.'

His hands tightened on her waist as his dark eyes continued to hold hers.

'London isn't Soria,' he said briefly, although he didn't let her go. 'Cathy, I have a lot to say to you,' he added, steadying her on her feet, 'but it must wait until we return to Soria.'

Teresa, who had been an interested spectator, jumped back into the cart.

'I'll take this food down to the men,' she suggested, laying the rein along the pony's back to start him off. 'See you when you come!'

Before they had time even to protest the cart was rolling and bumping its way downwards over the land which might have been destroyed by flood but which lay now in the early morning sunlight, as rich and fertile as it had always been.

Jaime turned to find his horse. The patient animal had been cropping the grass nearby, waiting for him to ride back to the makeshift camp which had been established at the foot of the valley, and something about its smooth whiteness reminded Catherine of another horse which was as black as ink.

'Lucía,' she said. 'What happened to her, Jaime? She left Soria to come up here—to be with you.'

His face darkened at the mention of his sister-in-law's name.

'She got here around one o'clock, apparently, after I had seen you safely on your way home.' He had used the word naturally, but he was still frowning. 'Cathy, all this is very painful to me, but it was Lucía who put the ruby in your room. She is a member of my family and I have to apologise for her, but it wouldn't surprise me if it is something you could never forgive.'

'Manuel told me.' Catherine's voice was not quite steady. 'He said Lucía had offered him the ruby, but he had given it back. Jaime,' she added breathlessly, 'please don't let us talk about it any more. I know you had nothing to do with it and that's all that really matters. Lucía's home is at Soria——'

'Not any more,' he said, tight-lipped. 'I have asked her to go. She will be provided for elsewhere, of course. I offered her Las Rosas, but she would not accept it. The isolation, she said, would be too great, so now it will await Ramón and Alex Bonnington if they care to use it when they marry. As for Lucía,' he continued harshly, 'she will probably go back to Madrid where my grandmother will keep an eye on her till she marries again.'

Tired though he undoubtedly was, he had fulfilled his responsibilities to his family as carefully as he could, providing even for Lucía until she married for a second time.

'She will not return to Soria,' he said unexpectedly. 'She has gone to the Serranos in the meantime and she will wait there till her possessions are sent to her.' He drew a quick breath. 'This was something I didn't mean to say to you until we were back at Soria, Cathy, but now I know that it will not keep.' His voice was suddenly vibrant with passion. 'I love you. I've wanted you ever since you proved how wrong I was about your youth back there in Madrid. For a long time I've known I had to keep you here, not only for Teresa's sake but for my own, yet I couldn't believe that you would stay. You have made a difference in all our lives —Teresa's and Ramón's and mine—and Soria needs you. I never thought to be in love again,' he added slowly, 'but I knew that night when I saw you with the wedding *mantilla* on your head and the petals from the floss-silk tree on the ground at your feet. Cathy!' He put his arms about her. 'Even after all that has happened, after everything Lucía has done and my utter blindness, will you marry me?'

She could not believe that he had asked her so simply, his proud head bent to catch her answer, and then all the joy of loving and being loved in return rose in her heart to be reflected in her shining eyes.

'Jaime,' she said, 'there's nothing I wouldn't do to make you happy. Surely you know that?'

'No,' he said, 'I would never have guessed. Not in the beginning, anyway!' He was smiling down at her in the golden light. 'Nothing that happens from now on will ever dismay me,' he declared. 'I have paid Lucía back Soria's debt to her and I am a poor man, but soon the *hacienda* will prosper and we will live well. Ramón, I think, will stay at Las Rosas, but that is for Alex to decide.'

He took her fully into his arms and their lips met in a long, promising kiss which was so utterly different from the kiss he had taken on the day of *fiesta*.

'What will your parents say to all this?' he asked, true to his sense of family obligation. 'Do you think they are likely to object to me?'

'On the contrary,' Catherine said with a wry little smile, 'I think they'll be relieved to know I've found someone to look after me.'

Once more he kissed her, holding her close as his eagle gaze swept down across the terraces lying tranquilly in the sun to the ragged banana plantations below.

'All this,' he said, 'and love, too! It was indeed worth waiting for, Cathy. The past is now behind me and the future is very bright.'

The patient white Arab nuzzled his arm.

'Time to go!' he said, lifting her easily into the saddle. 'There's still much work to be done.'

They rode down towards the valley, the tall man on the white stallion with the slight, bright-haired English girl seated behind him, her arm loosely about his waist. It was a scene as old as time in the mountains, a man and a woman setting out on a journey which would last a lifetime.

Harlequin Plus

A WORD ABOUT THE AUTHOR

Jean S. MacLeod was born in Glasgow, starting life with a "built-in love for Scotland." Such a statement comes as no surprise to her thousands of faithful readers who share that built-in love through such Romances as *My Heart's in the Highlands* (#1711) and *Master of Glenkeith* (#1291).

Jean spent her youth traveling in the footprints of heroes of Scottish literature, "storing, unconsciously, material for my first novel." Her father was a fount of information on all things Scottish—also a big help in her later writing.

During World War II she helped guard the Holy Loch, a British submarine base in Scotland, and while waiting for her husband to complete his wartime service, she wrote several books, which were sold as serials to a popular Scottish women's magazine. "These were years of stress," Jean explains. "But they were also years of growing."

After the war Jean and her family settled in Yorkshire, England. Her books began appearing on the stands regularly and she began to travel. "The fascination of visiting new and distant places gave me authentic backgrounds for more novels set abroad. But always there was a demand for Scottish stories."

Today she and her husband live on an isolated peninsula in Scotland's Western Highlands, and from her doorstep is a breathtaking panorama of the Hebrides. Primroses, violets, bluebells and tiny marsh orchids grow in glorious profusion all around. "In these surroundings," she says, "it must surely be possible to go on writing for a very long time."

What the press says about Harlequin romance fiction...

"When it comes to romantic novels...
Harlequin is the indisputable king."
—*New York Times*

" 'Harlequin [is]...the best and the biggest.' "
—*Associated Press* (quoting Janet Dailey's husband, Bill)

"The most popular reading matter of
American women today."
—*Detroit News*

"...exciting escapism, easy reading, interesting
characters and, always, a happy ending....
They are hard to put down."
—*Transcript-Telegram*, Holyoke (Mass.)

"...a work of art."
—*Globe & Mail*, Toronto

FREE!
Romance Treasury

**A beautifully bound,
value-packed,
three-in-one
volume of romance!**

Romance Treasury

An exciting opportunity to collect treasured works of romance! Almost 600 pages of exciting romance reading in each beautifully bound hardcover volume!

You may cancel your subscription whenever you wish! You don't have to buy any minimum number of volumes. Whenever you decide to stop your subscription just drop us a line and we'll cancel all further shipments.